THE NIGHTMARE MAN

A RUSSIAN ZOMBIE NOVEL
MICK FRANKLIN

SEVERED PRESS
HOBART TASMANIA

THE NIGHTMARE MAN

THE NIGHTMARE MAN

The frozen wasteland extended for hundreds of miles in all directions, over hills and through a surprisingly high population of trees. Snow clung to the leaves and branches, dripping like foam, the ground completely covered in thick ice. The sun was astonishing, the sky clear in places and curdled with clouds in others, an almost aching and peaceful beauty. A photo of Siberia would have looked romantic, adventurous. The reality was dangerous. The harsh cold tried to destroy the alien structure in this place; no thing was welcome here.

The building was a prison.

The prison itself was built for purpose, not beauty, and it still had Communist symbols and even a statue of Stalin before it, even though Communism had been gone from Mother Russia for seventy years. The windows were all barred, but that was not unusual in Russia. A cold wind blew around the building, worsening the minus thirty-eight-degree temperature. It even hurt to breathe.

A line of prisoners marched out to a point a hundred metres away from the main building. They were closely followed by the guards, who were strong men in clean uniforms and the Russian *sharpka*, or trapper hats, their boots crushing the snow beneath them. Their eyes held no empathy and were as cold and relentless as the bitter horizon, their gaze unflinching beneath the falling snow. The guards did not even look directly at their prisoners. Behind them came two more men; one was The Colonel, who was in charge of the prison. He was a large man, sometimes called Medved, or The Bear. He was the only person grinning. Beside him was a much smaller man called Anton.

"You see, my friend," The Bear gestured to the wilderness stretching off in every direction. "No need for walls."

Anton carefully studied the white wastelands, although he had seen them many times before, holding his hands together. He had two pairs of gloves on. Anton looked to The Bear.

1

"No prisoner can survive out there," The Colonel continued. "He can escape, but that's not the point. Getting out of my prison is the easy part. No, his real problems start when he gets away from my prison. There's literally nothing out there. A distance so vast that it would take months to cross it. And there are wild animals out there."

"Wild animals?"

"Bears, for one thing. And tigers. Not to mention the various hunters and trappers out there. Now, you would think they would help an escaped prisoner, right? A man who is the 'underdog,' a victim of a cruelly oppressive system, probably even a fellow Christian, a man who for all intents and purposes is just like them, just less fortunate. Am I right? Of course I am. But they have learned not to help any prisoner. They too have been educated."

Anton didn't look at The Colonel. Instead, he paid attention to the front of the column which had stopped moving. Two guards seized the lead man and dragged him away from the group. His hands were bound with a zip-tie and he fell to his knees when the guards released him. Anton could see that this man had a blanket around him.

"How do you mean 'educated,' exactly?" Anton asked.

The Colonel laughed. "Not like these poor souls you see here! But still, they got the point. It is not too wise to hide a prisoner from us. No, not a good idea at all. You too will receive an education while you are here –"

Anton turned to him sharply.

"But not in the same way, of course! No, I promised your mother I would help you get a respectable position in the prison service. She would never forgive me if anything was to happen to you."

Anton was squinting his eyes against the intrusive cold. He still found this place difficult to cope with, even though he had a lifetime familiarity with Russian winters.

"What are they doing with that prisoner up there?"

"Let's take a closer look!" The Colonel led the way.

A rough circle of people formed around the man kneeling in the snow. The guards were spread out, hands clutching rifles to their chests, a tactical distance kept between them and the prisoners.

"And here we find ourselves …" The Bear addressed the man crouched in the snow; there was no other sound but the wind. The man waited. The Bear looked off somewhere in the distance. "Are you sorry for what you have done?"

In what seemed to take a very long time the man lifted his head to look at The Colonel. He had one hand holding the frayed edges of his blanket together, keeping the hungry cold out, and Anton realized the man had nothing on beneath that blanket.

"I am … sorry," said the prisoner.

"Well, my friend," The Colonel stomped forward in a comical manner, he clasped his hands behind his back and leant closer to the prisoner, "Sorry just isn't fucking good enough this time."

At once, the two guards behind the prisoner ripped his blanket away, holding it up high as though he might try to jump to reach it. The prisoner hugged himself fiercely, squeezing himself into a ball. The cold was like a living thing greedily licking at his stacked ribs and skinny limbs, seizing him from all directions.

"You see, I'm not going to educate just you, I'm going to educate fucking everybody."

A second guard rushed to The Colonel's side, his face lean and brutal. He was tiny beside The Colonel, but strong. He held a wooden pale in his gloved hands. It was brimming with water.

Anton opened his mouth to scream, knowing what was about to happen and trying to stop it, his voice beginning and dying as the water was cast from the bucket, a giant silver plume in the air colliding with the prisoner's chest as he reared back in horror. He had time for his own agonized scream as the water did its work, freezing almost instantly, trapping him in a pose of a man pleading with God.

The ice on his body began to turn the prisoner's body blue, and Anton remembered a stupid American video game that had been unrealistic but fun to play, where one of the fighters in the game had the ability to freeze people with an ice blast from his hands, and then he could walk up to them and punch them. In the game, the unfortunate person who had been frozen was stuck inside their ice prison for a few seconds before they could shake it off and be free. The prisoner did not have that option.

Anton's mouth hung open, his heart was racing and he didn't know what to do. He was hardly aware of the other prisoners sharing his horror, or of the guards who seemed indifferent.

"Hammer," The Colonel called out, and instantly, another guard marched up to him with a hammer, placing it in his hand as though he was about to perform life-saving surgery.

The Colonel adjusted his grip slightly, finding the balance of the taped handle. He walked up to the frozen statue, gaining velocity as he moved, rearing his arm back for a giant swing.

The hammer clashed with the frozen prisoner who shattered like glass. Fragments of a human being sparkled and fell in the snow. The top half of his body was gone, smashed away, and as the final pieces fell, Anton watched in silence.

The Colonel turned away, and as he walked, he clapped an arm around Anton, making him walk with him. The prisoners were also rounded up by the guards and led back towards the prison building. The Colonel was smiling beneath his moustache and his head was held high.

"You see why we don't have a fucking discipline problem in my prison?"

***

Anton had a small room in the office area of the prison. It was functional and quiet, and at least the cold didn't get in here. The plumbing and electrical wiring were visible on the walls. A small barred window looked out on the frozen courtyard. There were several people in furs outside working and moving vehicles, but Anton didn't watch them. He was reading through his psychology books instead. The bunk bed above where he lay reading held his suitcases because there was not enough room to put them anywhere else. His jacket hung in the skinny closet. A small cracked mirror hung from its door.

Turning the page delicately, he sighed deeply. He had lost any concentration he was going to have today, and he felt it might even be a week before he could get into a book again. His mind kept snatching back to the unfortunate incident outside, the one where he had seen a man killed. He had no idea what the man had done to receive such a harsh punishment or even what the man had been a prisoner for. In the end, he felt that didn't matter – the man had been treated brutally beyond all reason and there was no justification for that. This was a modern-day civilized society.

Placing the book on his chest, he put his hands behind his head and thought deeply. Did he really even want to be here anymore? His uncle was obviously a severe man who was not shy about enforcing discipline. Perhaps that was necessary in a place like this, in order to keep the most dangerous criminals in line and prevent them from becoming violent, but Anton didn't like it. He didn't know what the answer was, but there had to be something better than what he had witnessed this morning. What did he hope to gain from being here? A valuable insight to the criminal mind, some work experience that would look impressive on his record and show that he was more than just a "theory man" trained by the university; he was someone who knew what he was talking about and had interacted with criminals firsthand.

He put the book very carefully beside him – like all his books, it had cost him a lot of money, a lot of which had come from working as a waiter at "Pizza Mania." Any time he ever went back to that place, he always tried to leave a small tip. The person serving him would always frown, surprised, but Anton insisted they take the money. After all, he remembered all too well what it was like struggling to get by. Now, of course, thanks to an education fund set up by his grandfather, Anton had enough money to live comfortably. The education fund had become his only when he turned twenty-one, but it meant he could really concentrate on his studies instead of living hand to mouth and month to month. That made the world of difference. And so, when he went into Pizza Mania as a customer, he would order a gourmet pizza and smoke a sheesha, maybe even drink some pivo or whiskey while he studied a book or chatted with a university friend, and he always made a point of tipping the staff.

Could he really stay here for another three months with his psychopathic uncle? What he had witnessed this morning was a type of brutality he had never even heard about before. No matter what the prisoner in question had done, freezing him and executing him like that had to be the most brutal thing Anton had ever witnessed. So what was he going to do? March into The Bear's office and tell him he had had enough? That he was leaving? He had one thing in his favour and that was that he was related to The Bear, so The Bear might actually say yes and send him home immediately, but what if he said no? Anton still had another three months placement out here, and he had no doubts at all that The Bear could make that time extremely unpleasant for him indeed if he wished, especially if he felt that Anton had disrespected him in his own house.

The best and most realistic option was to try and formulate some other reason for leaving; a family emergency, perhaps. He would need to leave it at least a week or two first, to make it look as though his reason for leaving was completely unrelated to the incident out in the yard. Maybe he could call his mother and explain what was going on, or at least that he was sick of this place and wanted to come home. She loved him with all her heart and would deny Christ three times for him if that's what it meant to make her son happy. She would support any story that he told to The Bear.

Anton took the door handle in his hand. It felt frail. Dimly, he felt vibrations from the door, the result of some manual work going on somewhere in the prison. He opened the door and headed to the cafeteria. A coffee and a small meal would help ease his nerves.

***

His meal was borsch soup and dumplings which he ate with a large *loshki*, or spoon. The dumplings weren't bad, but they were the instant stuff – he had certainly eaten better. Having his meal, Anton watched the other staff. They wore woolen jumpers and many of them had their hats on even inside, because this part of the prison wasn't heated. Close by, a guard in a jacket and *sharpka* hat was drinking from a cup of noodles and reading a cheap war comic, something you might pick up for a few rubles in a convenience store. For some reason he didn't understand, this made Anton sad.

The furniture was basic but functional, like most of the prison. There were a lot of repairs to be done that just weren't seen as urgent; here, the linoleum floor was torn away, revealing aged wood beneath, there, the pistachio-coloured paint on the ceiling had peeled away to show the green surface that used to be there, and elsewhere, the piping and electrical cables on the outside of the walls needed attention.

The lighting inside this great room was minimal, concentrated on the serving area where several prisoners silently dished up food according to what the staff ordered. Anton felt a rush of panic seeing the prisoners walking around free like that – if they were working in the kitchen, then surely they had access to knives and rolling pins and other similar weapons? It would be quite easy for them to overwhelm the staff in this room and then from here spread out in a rebellion, and quite possibly take over the entire prison. He could imagine that would be quite easy even with just a little planning – the prisoners could all seize a knife out of the kitchen and then attack the guards in this room, killing them all before the alarm could be raised, maybe keeping a few alive as hostages if they needed to negotiate later on. From there, they could spread out and make their way to the cells, opening each cell door and liberating the prisoners inside, quickly building up their ranks and turning the tide in their favour.

Of course, there were lockdown procedures and sturdy doors between every part of the prison, and only the most obedient prisoners were given duties such as working in the kitchens. Still, Anton couldn't help being afraid of the prisoners.

Anton watched the prisoners more closely. The prisoners who prepared and served the food and brought the guards coffee all had a defeated look about them. Not one of them would look the guards in the eyes. They did their job and no more, barely speaking even to each other.

Anton thought of the prisoner who had been killed this morning, his body frozen and then shattered into a thousand pieces. He didn't think that insubordination would be a real problem here; no one wanted to risk be killed like that. The example had been set and the message understood by everyone. Even those who hadn't seen would learn very soon what had happened this morning out in the snow. Disturbingly, he wondered if The Bear might actually have used a legitimate method for keeping control over the prisoners.

He sipped his coffee. It was weak and tasted vaguely like metal. He had gotten it from the machine. Grimacing from the coffee, he made a mental note to ask around for some real tea. All kinds of goods were up for trade here, especially since the postal service in Russia was an embarrassment and it was so difficult to get luxury items brought in. It was common for people to trade items with each other, even between prisoners and guards, although that was against procedure. Anton had been surprised that cold cash meant very little here ... but some cough lozenges or chocolate bars seemed to take on the value of gold. He had traded one set of extra woolen mittens for some soft cheese wrapped in brown paper and string and a small flask of vodka. It had been a guilty pleasure to sit in his room at night and enjoy them.

A moment after Anton placed his cup on the table, a big hand clapped him on the back.

"Ah, nephew! How are you liking it here?"

Anton looked up to see The Bear accompanied by two guards. The two guards were stone-faced, neutral, relaxed but predatory.

"Very well, thanks. I've been tending to my studies and I stepped out to get a coffee."

"Well, you can come with us while I do my rounds. You can see where the real prisoners are kept, the ones we don't want mixing with the general crowd."

Anton had picked his coffee up again, "I really just came out for a quick break, I should be –"

"Nonsense! You'll learn a lot more from real life than you ever will from a textbook. Get that coffee down and I'll show you the real world, how it really is. You won't want to miss it."

Anton considered the coffee for a moment. Despite his fear of The Bear, he was still curious to see who these prisoners were, the ones who were kept away from everyone else. He swirled his coffee once and put it back on the table. Then stood to join The Bear on his rounds. Besides, he didn't really have a choice, did he?

***

They walked through a corridor that seemed to belong to a different prison entirely. Here, there were old stone walls, and if the wiring had been bad before, then here it was positively dangerous. A number of lights had burned out and were waiting to be replaced. The floor wasn't even, but seemed to gradually descend, as if they were making their way underground to some ancient chambers. For all Anton knew, they were. Once, he brushed his hand along the soft stone edges of the wall. He felt a chill through him, as though the wind had somehow found its way into this ancient part of the prison.

The Bear led the way with Anton closely behind. The two guards walked shoulder to shoulder. Anton found he could barely tell them apart. The doors here were heavy studded iron, set into the walls with thick brackets and held by large locks. The Bear stopped by the first door and grinned through the barred window of the door. Then he moved aside. Anton hesitated a moment, somehow expecting that if he got too close to the door, a hand would reach out and grab him – he had no doubt that all the prisoners feared The Bear, but they would recognize instantly that Anton was soft, an easy target. He moved closer to the door.

Inside, the cell was lit by grey light that came in from a long way up in the ceiling. Dust motes swam in the chambered light. The walls were bare, some patches of paint clung to the brickwork in many places. For some reason, there was a raised section of brickwork on the floor, almost like a pedestal of some sort, although more likely it had served another purpose when this building had been in other hands. There was no bed in this section, just some straw laid out on the floor with some rags and old sacks that served as blankets and a pillow. The cell's one occupant looked as surprised to see Anton as he was to see the prisoner. Anton shared a moment looking into The Bearded skinny man's eyes. The Bear's voice beside him almost made him scream.

"Doesn't look like much, does he? No, you wouldn't expect much from one that looks so weak, would you? And yet it's funny to think, he's in there for a very good reason."

The Bear moved away, apparently not concerned about imparting the reason why the skinny man was locked up.

"Why *is* he in there?" Anton couldn't resist asking.

The Bear answered instantly, "He beat his wife to death with her own artificial leg. I've certainly seen worse things, but something about this man's crime sickened even me. So I put him where he is now. Away from the other prisoners. Now he won't be able to hurt anybody."

Anton glanced into the cell again. The prisoner had changed his position on the floor. His eyes were wide as if he could understand nothing of what was being said.

"And who was he before?" Anton said, still looking at the prisoner.

"A shoe salesman," The Bear said without looking back. "He snapped quite unexpectedly, quoting the reason for the murder was that his life revolved around selling people two shoes, and he couldn't bear having a wife with only one foot. He was just a normal man living with the daily struggles of a normal life, struggling to put bread on the table. Then one night he lost it. Went totally out of his mind."

The Bear paused for a moment, considering. Then he turned on Anton, standing at his full height, one finger raised threateningly. Anton shrank against the wall. All his life, it seemed, he had been a scared man. Now, he expected The Bear to tell him off, something like, "Listen, you little shit, I know you're thinking of leaving. Well, if you even try, I'm giving you a cell like that guy you see in there. Then you'll really know what it means to want to be free from here. See, this is the real reason for our little journey underneath the prison."

Instead, The Bear said, "Do not let these guys control you. I know you're an educated person, you're book smart, but in here is a different world. These people are in here because this is exactly the right place for them. It's a constant assault; they are constantly trying to feel you out, to sense any weakness.

Anything they do for you is not free. It will be used as leverage against you at some point. And then before you know it, you are smuggling drugs in here for them. I had one officer who even brought in a fucking guard uniform for a prisoner, who planned to escape. Can you fucking believe it? Fucking outrageous. I questioned the officer, and as it turns out, it all began with little things – he felt sorry for the prisoner so he started bringing him in biscuits, which is not a big thing, but he was doing it without openly confirming it with his supervisor. That's clearly against procedure. Straight away, the prisoner knew he had something over this man, that he was weak, that he would let the small things slide.

So then the prisoner kept on working on him, gradually getting the officer to do more and more small things for him, until eventually one day, the prisoner said to him, 'Listen, motherfucker, you are going to bring an officer's uniform in for me. I'm leaving this place at the shift change. If you don't do exactly as I say, I will kill you. Besides, I've kept track of every rules violation you've made – even if I don't kill you, you will definitely lose your job.'

From the officer's point of view, this came out of nowhere, but actually, the prisoner had been setting this up for nearly a year. He had taken an inch at a time in order to get a mile."

"Did you get the prisoner back?" Anton asked.

The Bear laughed. He continued the tour.

The guards stepped forward in tandem, and Anton hurried to catch up to The Bear. The next cell had even less light. With more confidence this time, Anton looked through the barred window.

An older man sat against the wall. He carried some extra weight, looking overweight but very strong. He wore a cheap brown jacket and two shirts underneath. His mouth seemed to have an unconscious twitch, constantly resetting itself like a fat bird that couldn't get comfortable on its perch.

"This is some guy," said The Bear with a voice that suggested amazement. "He murdered forty-six people! A mass murderer. He went undetected for years, killing people in his own apartment. It was mostly homeless people he killed, but eventually, when he killed his landlady, the police took an interest in him. I told her family I would never let him out of there. So far, I kept my word."

Anton looked at the prisoner again. The prisoner breathed with difficulty and kept on moving slightly against the wall, looking as if he was dozing off and then being startled awake again. From one of his shirts, two cockroaches crawled out. Anton moved on.

The Bear spoke to Anton as they walked. "Don't let them call you by your first name. In one hundred percent of the cases where prisoners have gotten the better of guards, the prisoner had been allowed to use the guard's first name. It doesn't sound like a big thing, but if you allow it to happen, it signals you are weak, and you can be worked on.

Here's some real world psychology right here; if a prisoner breaks the rules even slightly, you need to be on it immediately. It's all a test, you see. And the prisoner actually respects you for keeping him in line. Everyone feels safer that way."

Anton glanced into one cell, curious to see its occupant, but this cell was empty.

When Anton caught up to The Bear, he saw that the large man had his teeth bared. He quite clearly did not like the occupant of the next cell. Anton felt a trickle of fear, unconsciously taking a step behind The Bear. He was glad he wasn't the man inside the cell. The Bear gave the introduction.

"This motherfucker was involved in the Novgorod bombing. That's right; he's a fucking terrorist against the Russian people."

Disgustedly, The Bear turned on his heel and stormed off.

Anton looked through the bars and saw a surprisingly young man there. The young man's face was mostly blank but Anton saw something else … contempt? It was Anton who looked away first. He moved on with the tour.

The Bear had stopped before the next door. He hesitated. It was only a fraction of a second, and yet to Anton, it seemed a very long time. In that moment, Anton saw not fear, but a small doubt in The Bear's mind, something that had pierced his confidence. It was the only time Anton had ever seen that. That slight pause also made Anton think just how much he depended on The Bear for his own safety.

The Bear said, "This man is someone very special."

He left the words in the air. Anton felt no need to break the silence. Anton saw that there were numbers embedded on this steel door. Leaning closer, he could see that the prison door numbers were 64389000. Inside was a man sitting against the stone wall whose clothes were almost rags. His wild hair hung past his eyes and his head had fallen forward to his knees. Snaggles of hair grew from his beard, his hair black and full of dirt. His hands and feet were bandaged and covered in grime as if he was just finished a shift in the coal mines. The prisoner had no fat on him, but his build was wiry and it looked like he had once been very strong. There was no reaction at all from him when The Bear had spoken.

"They call him the Nightmare Man," The Bear said with some satisfaction. "He's the most fucking dangerous guy in here."

Anton looked into the cell again, imagining for a split second that this prisoner would have somehow crossed the distance of the cell to snake out a hand between the bars and murder him. But the prisoner hadn't moved. He seemed slumped and powerless, an empty vessel.

The Bear hadn't taken his eyes off the prisoner. Somewhere in The Bear's face, Anton saw … what? Admiration? It was probably a trick of the light, although later he would have reason to wonder.

"We let him out only when he needs medical attention. And occasionally for some sunlight. But even then, he has his hands and feet shackled and he is escorted by four guards. We don't take any chances with that one."

"That's some name," Anton said. The Bear turned his head quizzically.

"The Nightmare Man, I mean," said Anton. "I guess he must have done something terrible to earn it."

"You guess right, kid. This guy's like something you've never even read about."

"Is there anyone waiting for him outside? I mean, does he have family?"

"Only one family member left, apparently. His brother."

The Bear suddenly grinned and slapped his hand against the cell door as if the prisoner couldn't hear them and he was trying to get his attention. The Bear said to the prisoner, "You thought your brother was lost for a very fucking long time, didn't you? Well guess what, your brother's been found! He's turned up and I know where he is. Isn't that some good news for you?"

Very slowly, the Nightmare Man lifted his head. His expression was so sad that for a moment Anton forgot that he was seeing a psychopath, a man who was likely locked up in isolation for very good reason. The prisoner's eyes were black, and Anton could see this man had been utterly destroyed. Whatever The Bear had done to him had annihilated what he was … and yet he wasn't completely defeated, because Anton saw twin sparks of life in those eyes, distant, dormant, but still there. He made no other reaction.

"Come on, let's go," The Bear said to Anton. "We've got other prisoners to see."

The Nightmare Man listened to them go. Their footfalls carried a very long way, mixed with chatter, and eventually, the heavy door at the end of the corridor slamming shut and being bolted. The noise was faint but final. He opened his hands and looked at them; they were weaker than they once were. But there was always potential.

He looked to the mangled blankets and straw that made up his bed. A steel bucket was in the corner of the cell for his waste. The window was high up on the wall, but reachable. He had not looked out through it in a long time, had not felt a need to. Now his eyes lifted to the light flooding in, as though it was something truly precious. Beside him was a steel plate with his meal. Moving very slowly, he began to eat. He would need to be strong.

That night, the Nightmare Man went back into training. He used the small brick pedestal in his room to perform sets of dips on and elevated push-ups. He struggled at first, shockingly weak, falling in a quivering heap on the floor after exercise, wet with perspiration and breathing raggedly. But gradually, over a number of weeks, his strength seemed to return so that he was doing push-ups on his fingertips. A few weeks later, he was doing handstand pushups, at first using the wall for support, eventually not even needing that. His legs grew stronger, becoming more toned, as he worked on one-legged squats, eventually adding in a jump to this movement.

He had heard that his brother was alive. It was all the reason the Nightmare Man needed to come to life again.

2.

Doctor Alastair was a criminal. He had been sent to the Siberian prison on charges of negligence, namely that he had taken morphine while he had been on duty at the hospital. The stress of being a doctor was incredible; he had needed some escape. The fact was that he could perform his duties just as well after a hit of morphine as what he did without it – he would never have endangered innocent lives if he didn't believe this was the case. He certainly wasn't the only one who was taking drugs, but he had been the only doctor to be stripped of his licence and given a lengthy prison sentence. Even though it had been the only time he had taken morphine and been on shift, the judge still said he had abused the public trust, and for that, he had to pay. And pay he had. The prison was a constant reminder of his shame. He was a disgrace. But on the positive side, The Bear had appointed Alastair the prison doctor, so he got to run the clinic, which was in a separate building to the main prison. This building was quite well lit, although the paint was still peeling off the walls and the exposed wiring and pipes could do with some maintenance work. Alastair got to sleep out here in his own room and pretty much had the run of the prison just so long as he was always available to see any person who was sick.

Alastair picked up his clipboard, moving closer to the window for more light. He froze when he saw the next name on his list to be seen; the name was Kirill.

"Excuse me," a guard called out from the doorway, halted at the threshold. The man was strong; he should have been a soldier, or a sambo champion.

"Yes?" Alastair asked.

"I have your next patient here," the guard said, nodding respectfully, even though Alastair was still technically a prisoner. The guard stepped aside and revealed the prisoner known as the Nightmare Man.

Doctor Alastair regarding this patient for a moment. "That's fine, you can leave me with him."

"Okay, I'll be just down the hall."

The Nightmare Man waited until Doctor Alastair motioned for him to enter the room, and sit on the bed. The patient moved slowly, but there was a definite strength about him, like a relaxed tiger ready to switch on at a moment's notice. The Nightmare Man sat on the bed and fixed his gaze at the wall, not looking at Doctor Alastair.

"So, how are you feeling?" Alastair asked.

Kirill's eyes drifted to the surgical tools laid out on the bench, a mixture of scalpels, his eyes stayed on them – too long – before meeting Alastair's.

"Fine."

"Good, good. You're looking well."

Kirill looked slowly out the window and then back at the door.

"So," Alastair began, "I need to check your blood pressure and pulse, and I will also do some basic blood tests –"

"I need out."

Alastair paused.

"Goddamnit! Why would you tell me that?"

In what seemed like a split second, the guard was at the door. His expression was gently quizzical, but his hand had gone to the firearm on his belt.

"It's okay," Alastair told him. "Sorry, the prisoner made an inappropriate remark. I've never liked dirty jokes. But it's fine. I'll continue with my examination. Thank you, I appreciate your concern, I really do."

The guard nodded once and was away, but his hand didn't stray from the firearm.

Alastair leaned closer. "Okay, I can help you … but I've got to ask, how do you plan to cross Siberia? That's one of the most dangerous places in the world out there."

The Nightmare Man said, "You didn't ask me why. But I'll tell you. The Bear said he knows that my brother is alive. I heard him say this myself. All I need to do is get The Bear alone –"

"Forget it, I don't want to hear this. You either make your escape without hurting anyone, or I will have nothing to do with this. If I tell The Colonel what you just said, he will never let you out of your cell, no matter what your condition."

"That's true. But I would really like your help."

"Not a fucking chance. No one gets hurt. That's the condition. If you can agree to that, then I will talk to you about getting out of here. Otherwise, rot in your cell. It's no skin off my nose."

The Nightmare Man nodded. "Okay. I won't kill anyone before I'm outside the prison. Good enough?"

Alastair nodded slowly. "Promise me. Swear that no one will get hurt."

Kirill said without emotion, "No one will get hurt. I promise."

Satisfied, Alastair put his hands in his gown pockets.

"But I still need some way of finding my brother …"

"Yes, your brother. I see." Alastair appeared in deep concentration. "I will try my best to get this information from The Bear. Maybe he will tell me. If not, you will just need to go home, do some detective work there. I'm sure a man with your persuasiveness will get answers."

The Nightmare Man said, "Home."

"It's Chelyabinsk, isn't it? Where you're from? That's where you'll go."

Kirill nodded. "Yeah. I'll start there. Someone's got to know something."

Alastair opened a cupboard door and hauled out a canvas backpack. It was quite large with many pouches that were buckled closed. It was obviously full of equipment.

"Well, as you don't seem to have any plan to escape, you will need this!" Alastair announced proudly, "I have put together an escape kit. It's everything a man would need to cross Siberia. It's taken me years to put this stuff together." He patted the bag like it was a loyal dog.

"Were you thinking of escaping?"

"Me? No, I don't think I have the constitution to survive out there. But a guy like yourself, you could do this. I've got a compass to give you and a map. Just head due south; you'll be in Chelyabinsk before you know it."

Doctor Alastair put the backpack into the cupboard again in case the guard returned.

Kirill said, "Then my biggest problem will be the people pursuing me. There is no way The Bear will just let me go. He'll have every fucking *politsia*, eskimo, hunter, and KGB agent he knows looking for me. I need some way to throw him off my trail. Or even better, lose him entirely."

"You will have heard the rumours about how they killed Calder outside a few months ago? They threw water over him so he froze, then they smashed him."

"I heard, yes."

"Well, I insisted he have a Christian burial."

Alastair gestured for Kirill to stand up and look out the window. Outside, there was a grave with a cross made from two branches lashed together with a strip of leather. Kirill gazed at the grave for long moments. Then he understood.

3.

Anton closed the book on psychology. It was night time now, his small room lit by a bare bulb that hung from the ceiling. The prisoners had their lights turned off by the guards at eight every night, but Anton was free to keep his room lights on, of course. He placed the textbook back on the pile of books at the back of the little desk and instead opened his diary to a blank page. He held a pen over the page, deciding what to write. What he really wanted to say was that he was afraid, afraid that The Bear would get him killed, that one of the prisoners would kill him, that a guard would kill him, that all this isolation, of being so far removed from everything he had ever known, that that would kill him. What he wanted to put to paper was a final message for his mum, in the hopes that somehow this diary would find its way to her in the event of him dying in this Siberian prison. He wanted to write that The Bear was a monster, that he was utterly inhuman towards these prisoners who had been placed under his care. In the end, he couldn't write a thing. The fear defeated him.

Anton pretended to open the textbook again. He pretended he was studying. He pretended that he wasn't a coward, and that he didn't hate himself. Not long after, he went to the top of his cupboard and took down a flask of vodka, it was a reasonable brand, something you might buy to share with a stranger, because it was a Russian custom to share hospitality to guests in their country. Opening a small leather pouch, Anton removed a tin shot glass from it. Expertly spinning the lid off the vodka, he poured a neat shot. It was gone in a second. If he was at home, he would have finished the bottle, but the unsettling reality that alcohol was difficult to attain out here made him feel uneasy and he returned the bottle to the top of the cupboard, pushing a jacket in front of it as if hiding the vodka from himself. It would only have made him feel worse tomorrow, anyway.

A book near the bottom of the stack caught his attention and Anton removed it, flipping it open to start reading. It was a training manual for prison guards who worked in the American prison service, and it was actually pretty good.

If Anton had turned to look out the window, he probably still wouldn't have noticed the lone person walking out of the prison, a prison with no walls, because it was surrounded by a vicious wilderness. The man was dressed head to foot in furs, prepared for a long march, carrying a broad backpack and disappearing into the night.

And if Anton had been watching a few minutes more, he may have seen a second person fled the prison that night, following the first man from a distance.

4.

The Nightmare Man walked all night. He was keen to put as much distance between him and the prison as he possibly could and as quickly as possible. Although Doctor Alastair's plan made sense, he had to take it that the plan would fail, that The Bear would see through it instantly and be in pursuit. It was also wise to assume that Doctor Alastair would betray him and tell The Bear everything. If Kirill assumed the worst, he would be more careful and increase his chances of surviving.

It wasn't until close to dawn that he finally set his backpack down. There was foam duct-taped to the straps so that they did not dig into his shoulders while he carried the pack. The pack itself had modest but adequate equipment divided into different sections of the bag. One pouch was dedicated to fire lighting, another was basic medical equipment, another was for simple shelter and included strong cord and waterproof sheets. He had tablets for water purification, water filters, as well as many other items.

The plan was for him to travel by night and sleep in the day. As long as he was clever in finding a hiding place to sleep in, he had a good chance of avoiding the patrols that he had to assume were being sent out after him. The local hunters and *eskimosis* would know this land far better than him, so he deliberately chose the less obvious routes, choosing to keep within the tree line where possible, walking over difficult terrain even when there was a suitable path available, trekking across a mountain when he could have traversed flat ground.

Although his destination, the city of Chelyabinsk, was almost due south, he planned to take an indirect route to get there. This would take more time and cost him more resources, but it was safer to assume that patrols were looking for him on the most direct route to the city. He would add a number of wide detours to his journey to try and lose any pursuers.

In the first light of dawn, he sat down among some trees, gazing out across the snowy landscape. While it didn't appear he would have a difficult walk tomorrow, it did seem there was nothing but emptiness in every direction. There were trees and the occasional animal, but no man-made structures of any kind, no city in the distance, not even a road.

Rummaging through the main compartment of the backpack, he took out a bottle of water and took several generous swigs. A lot of the weight of the backpack was water and food, which meant that he could save time by not having to go search for these things himself, and the further good news was that the backpack would progressively get lighter as he went on. When he had to, he could always resort to making his own water from snow or trying to catch his own food, but he hoped to put this off for as long as possible. By the time he ran out of supplies, he hoped to be close to some of the greenhouse farms that the immigrant Chinese used to grow and sell food to the Russians. He would be able to sneak in and steal food from the greenhouses easily enough.

There was also a small but sturdy knife in the backpack. Kirill's eyes widened, seizing the knife instantly. He drew it from its sheath, holding it up in the pale light, scrutinising its strength and effectiveness. It would do an adequate job of stabbing a man. And, of course, it would be useful for other duties such as cutting cords, carving tinder from branches, gutting any fish he might catch, and so on.

He hid himself as well as possible, using branches and gathering up mounds of snow. Hopefully, anyone looking through binoculars would not see a sleeping man there, but the disguise would likely fall apart if someone was walking close by.

He took a very deep breath, a breath of freedom. Then he settled down to sleep for the day. The knife was in his hand while he slept.

5.

The Bear listened to Doctor Alastair's story in silence. They were out in the frosted yard in front of the clinic, standing quite close to where there were two graves with crosses. The Bear had four guards with him and his nephew Anton.

"So you see," said Alastair, "Kirill was quite unwell. I know it seems sudden, but people die of pneumonia all the time."

"If anything, he seemed the picture of health to me," said The Bear. "I thought he was looking stronger than he had in a long time."

"I know it must seem strange, but I did keep you updated every day regarding his condition. He was sick for a number of weeks, as you obviously recall. He just wasn't getting any better."

"So you went ahead and buried him in the yard. Without even telling   me   first."
Alastair grimaced. "I'm sorry about that, sir; it's just that I believe in giving people a Christian burial. At the time, I saw no reason to wait. He was, after all, a dead body. I really didn't see what further possible use he could be to you."

"Hmm, he was quite a significant prisoner, you see. Normally, I don't give a shit if one of the prisoners dies, but that one ..."

Alastair held up his hands. "Sorry, sir, I wasn't aware. I have prepared the death certificate and a medical report if you would like me to put them on your desk."

A guard rushed up to The Bear. "Sir, excuse me."

"What is it?"

"We're missing a prisoner," said the guard, slightly out of breath.

"I know; Kirill. Doc Alastair just told me about him."

"Sir, I meant there is a prisoner missing from the clinic. I already knew about Kirill when I checked in with the doc in the morning, but then when I did roll call with the prisoners in the clinic, this guy didn't show up."

"You can't find him?"

"Well, we haven't searched everywhere. It's possible he may have gone back to his own cell, I guess. But I wanted to let you know immediately. I came here as soon as I realised he was gone."

The Bear turned to Doc Alastair. "Do you know anything about this second man? Why he can't be accounted for this morning?"

Doc Alastair shook his head. "I-I'm sorry, I hadn't even checked in on the patients this morning. If someone was missing, I honestly did not know."

"That's been quite an evening in the clinic. First of all, you had one of our most important prisoners die ... and you felt compelled to bury him, without even telling ME first that he was fucking dead. And then a second prisoner goes missing. Something isn't right here."

The Bear turned to the two graves; after a few moments, he looked at Doc Alastair again.

6.

Kirill awoke to darkness. His eyes calmly scanned as much as he could, trying to ascertain if there were any nearby threats. Eventually, he sat up slowly. The moon was bright in the sky. It would be a good evening for walking. He consulted his map again before starting his trek, also checking his compass to make sure he was definitely going in the right direction. He would veer slightly off course to confuse anyone who might be following him, and then check his bearings again. It sounded like a good plan.

Before he moved, he opened a tin of food from his pack. It was cold but edible. Briefly, he toyed with the idea of starting a fire, but almost instantly dismissed it – if he was being pursued (and it was in his best interest to assume that he was), then a fire would give him away to anyone for miles around. Sure, the fire would grant him great comfort and be a morale boost; he could even enjoy a cooked meal. But the risk of giving away his position was too much. He could do without a fire. Maybe when he got closer to

Chelyabinsk and he was genuinely in the clear, he could have a luxury such as a fire. For now, he would remain hidden.

So he ate the tinned food cold. It wasn't bad at all. He'd certainly eaten worse. He had a few drinks of water from a bottle, being careful not to spill any. Although he wanted to continue to put as much distance between the prison and himself as possible, he still took his time, making sure he was well fed and hydrated, that he had his map bearings correct, and that the pack was adjusted correctly.

He eventually began walking again, never walking on top of hills (he wanted to avoid presenting a silhouette to any observers), staying close to trees wherever possible, sometimes walking parallel to but never on roads. Frequently, he would turn and see if there were any pursuers, but he did not see a single soul that night.

The snow crunched beneath his boots, each step taking him closer to his brother. There was a nagging doubt that maybe The Bear had lied to him just to torment him – that there was no such news of his brother actually being alive. But Kirill had summoned the courage to leave the prison and risk The Bear's considerable wrath. He was free now, and he had to keep going. If Kirill was caught and dragged back to the prison, his time spent in the tiny primitive cell would seem like tickling compared to how The Bear would exact vengeance. It was likely he would not live to regret his escape.

Shortly before dawn, Kirill found a place to sleep for the coming day. He made a small tunnel in a mound of snow and covered the entrance with branches. Granted, there was not much room inside, but he felt he was well disguised from anyone who was walking outside.

He decided to use one of the two torches in the pack and look through the books he had been provided with. Kirill had told Doctor Alastair that the books would be a waste of space and weight, but Alastair had insisted, saying that they would prevent boredom and could always be used as fuel for starting fires, so Kirill had agreed to take them along.

Shielding the torchlight as much as possible with his fur coat, he looked through the titles. There was the first in the series of the Night Watch books, a series about a police force of wizards in

Moscow that looked after the witches, vampires, and werewolves there, as well as other bad wizards. There was Metro 2033, which was set after a global nuclear war and the apparent survivors were living in the metro system of Moscow.

The Nightmare Man stopped here. He held this book in a crushing grip as he read the back of it. The reason it affected him this way was that the last place his brother had been seen alive was in the Moscow metro system. There had been some indistinct footage of his brother staggering across an underground railway track, with two blurred people in the background, but there was little of any practical value in the video. Kirill had watched it in excess of one hundred times.

He placed the book down carefully. When he got a chance, he would read through it, even on the extremely unlikely chance that it would give him some clue about his brother's whereabouts. Next, there was Crime and Punishment, which was a fairly obvious choice.

Kirill decided to get some sleep. His pack was ready in case he had to flee at a moment's notice and his knife was always at hand.

Sleep came swiftly.

7.

The Nightmare Man awoke instantly.

Intruders.

He was already reaching for his knife, even as the adrenaline surged, he was still more angry than fearful – "Alright, you bastards, I'll fucking kill all of you."

Before leaping out of the snow cave, he paused, hearing a number of voices. Fucking hell, what to do? Had they seen his hiding place and were now closing in on him, or were they merely talking aloud and just happened to be in the area, and his best bet was simply staying right where he was?

The Nightmare Man bared his teeth, steeled to smash through the snow and start killing. He would bite and stab until they eventually shot him a hundred times – no less – and even then he would do his best to take them down with him.

Seething and *desperate* to kill, the Nightmare Man lay in wait.

… But it seemed the group outside had not seen him, for they moved on without incident. Kirill took many long minutes to calm down; the adrenalin had abandoned him and he felt weak, scared even. He also felt it best to let this group who had stumbled upon his hiding place depart with a clear distance between him and them before he set out again.

After his heart rate settled down, he gathered his backpack and quietly kicked away the branches blocking the entrance to the snow cave. Crouching outside, part of him was disappointed there had been no combat.

He looked about him, trying to find where the group was now, but enough time had passed for them to be gone.

Kirill still held the knife. The anger was still with him, also.

"Don't you dare," he said through gritted teeth, eyes blazing. "Don't you *ever* fucking dare sneak up on me …"

8.

Kirill was walking again. The sun low in the sky, the air cool to breathe. He had a scarf over his mouth because that made it easier to inhale the cold air. After his morning encounter with the strange group, he was extra alert, scanning his environment every few seconds. No way anyone was going to sneak up on him again.

His path led him to a valley between two mountains. He paused, quietly angry again – if he had checked his map properly, he could have anticipated this event, and found a different way around. Now his choices were walking through a valley – where he was hemmed in – or else backtrack considerably and find an alternate route, at the cost of much precious time.

Fuck this, he thought, I'm going through here.

The Nightmare Man marched between the mountains … and nothing happened. The journey seemed long; he expected danger at every moment, but there was simply nothing out there.

He stopped and evaluated his decision – in hindsight, he probably should have taken the time to find a longer way around and avoid a potential ambush, but the reality was that he was angry with himself for having been surprised that morning, and that had made him act aggressively, pressing ahead when the wisest decision would have been to take a longer but safer journey.

Still, he was here now.

He looked about him. There was a frozen lake, a great flat expanse. This type of scene was common in cities all over Russia, where rivers and lakes froze over for the winter, allowing people an additional path to walk across. Even Chelyabinsk had a river near Megapolis, the cinema and restaurant complex, which froze during the winter months and allowed free passage across it.

Given that no one had been waiting to ambush him in the valley he thought it was safe this time to walk across the frozen lake. Sure, it was flat, open ground, and normally, he did everything possible to avoid that type of terrain, but in this instance, he felt it was a direct path to where he wanted to go – there was little to lose by going directly ahead, because if anyone was laying in wait to ambush him, they would have done so already.

The Nightmare Man marched across the frozen lake. Yes, this was definitely the smart move. Had he skirted around the lake it would have taken him possibly hours, but this way he would easily be across the ice in no time, free to continue his journey and find a good resting place for the day.

Why, this way –

The ice began to crack.

Kirill froze, glancing left and right. He was in the middle of the lake; there was nowhere to run. If the ice gave in now, he would fall through, no matter how fast he ran. Why was the ice breaking now? Maybe because of the enormous backpack he was carrying. Who knew?

Trying to remain still as possible, Kirill heard another crack, and then that was it, it had stopped; false alarm after all, it looked like he was out of –

The ice shattered beneath him.

Kirill fell into the water; its suddenness ripping the air from his lungs savagely, he fell below the surface. His furs were wet, the heavy backpack, ordinarily a gift from God, was now an anchor dragging him down. With horrifying speed, he sank in the water, his limbs seizing up, his heart rate exploding through the stratosphere. It was one of his deepest fears – drowning.

He began to struggle out of the backpack, his arm getting snagged for a long moment until he fiercely shook it out, and he began to pump his limbs to drive himself to the surface, his lungs beginning to scream at him.

He smashed through the surface of the icy water, his hands coming down on the lip of the ice break. He was out, he was free –

To his horror, he began to black out and sink below the surface again.

Quickly taking a breath, his head began to sink below the water line.

The water rushed up his nose.

Don't fucking choke, you fool, his mind snarled at him, *or you'll drown.*

Kirill's inner monologue was a psychopath, cold as ice, hard as nails.

He resolutely drove his face at the hole in the ice, even as his body demanded that he choke and start inhaling water.

The Nightmare Man kicked and swam for the surface, smashing through the water once again, this time driving his knife down into the ice. It broke the ice … his salvation slid further away from him. Kicking himself towards the new edge that was created, he managed to get just his chest onto it, spreading his arms across the ice, distributing his weight as broadly as possible so as not to fracture the surface.

Darkness closed in again …

Back away, motherfucker, his mind spoke to the encroaching blackness. He began kicking his legs in the water, using that to slowly, slowly move onto the ice.

The darkness retreated enough for Kirill to haul himself up out of the water. His considerable strength and fitness allowed him to do this, although he was still utterly exhausted.

His breath came fierce, ragged. He was out of the water but not enough because he still dragged himself away further, fearful, in case he somehow slipped into the icy depths again.

"Fuck you," he whispered, then more savagely, "Fuck you."

He shivered violently. He couldn't stop. This was a coldness like he had never known. If he didn't fix this soon, all his problems would be over; he would die of hypothermia and nothing would matter.

With dismay, he realised he had left his backpack at the bottom of the lake. There was no physical way he could dive in there and retrieve it. After all, he had barely made it out alive *without* his backpack, let alone having its extra weight to hold him down.

His chances of survival had shrunk dramatically. With Doc Alastair's kit on his back, he probably could have marched all the way to Chelyabinsk comfortably. Now with barely anything on him, how was he supposed to survive out here?

Basically, he was dead.

But he was not the kind of man who gave up easily.

9.

"You're lucky you're the doctor here," said The Bear.

Alastair did not look up.

Kirill's supposed grave had been unearthed by two prisoners and was shown to be empty.

"You don't have anything to say for yourself?" The Bear asked. "You don't want to tell me that Kirill threatened you with your life, that he forced you to be in on his little plan?"

Alastair shook his head very slowly. Although the game was up, he clearly did not want to betray Kirill.

"That's fine," said The Bear. "I'm not going to turn you into ice and smash you, if that's what you were thinking I would do. It is almost impossible to get a doctor out here. But your sentence will certainly be extended. You may have helped Kirill escape, but you will definitely be here a long time."

The Bear turned to his guards. "We need whatever politsia, local hunters, and so on we can get involved. Anyone. Just make it extremely clear to everyone you speak to that the Nightmare Man is dangerous, and very much so. His little nickname suits him. He is not to be approached, unless they have a lot of guns pointed at him."

The guards nodded, two of them dispatching to begin calling for reinforcements in the manhunt.

The Bear turned to Anton. "I'm going out there myself. The guards can lockdown the prison, keep everyone in their cells. There's no way I'm not going to be out there. Would you like to come along?"

Anton nodded. "Sure, what's your plan?"

"I have some friends I can call. People who will be very interested in seeing Kirill caught again. That stupid fucker, his problems are only just beginning."

10.

Kirill was now on the opposite side of the lake, having found a fairly occluded section to set up camp. This section was not obvious from the main body of the lake, and was further hidden by snowdrifts and the natural slopes of the hills. In addition, Kirill took care to carve a small cave that was once again hidden from an inquisitive intruder who might investigate this place. So he had some respite, at least, from the savage cold.

He sat breathing heavily, his furs laid out in the sun to dry. The cold attacked him brutally, but his mind drove his body, and he put up with it – he could not sleep in wet clothes, because if he did, he might not wake up again. Normally, he considered it a risk to make a fire, but given that his clothes were soaked through, he felt he needed the fire to dry his clothes. Also, this area was fairly well secluded from view; he should be safe, just this once.

After searching his pockets, he had retrieved a few items of food; they were high-energy protein bars. They were, he felt, a poor substitute for the delicious tins of meat he had left at the bottom of the lake. Yet they were still a nutrition source. After a moment's thought, he decided to keep these energy bars in reserve – he would survive as long as he could without them, knowing all the time that he had something to fall back on if he genuinely needed it.

As his clothes dried, he stared savagely at the blade, something he had kept close to himself and ready at a moment's notice. The blade seemed to be a physical extension of his rage. He would express his anger through this tool.

He heard snow crunching. Someone was approaching.

The Nightmare Man crouched at the ready, naked but fully prepared to fight.

He closed in on the sound of approaching footsteps, assuming already the person knew he was here, but that they wouldn't expect him to be hunting them.

Taking care to move silently, he crept through the snow, blade drawn, determined to slaughter any aggressor he might find.

As the intruder set foot into the encampment, Kirill emerged from hiding. He froze. The intruder was a fellow prisoner, who must have been following him here.

"Kirill!" the man said.

"Humair," said Kirill. "You've escaped."

"Yeah! I saw you leave two nights ago. I was in the clinic as well, just for a chest infection. I saw you just pack up and leave! I couldn't believe it, my man."

A ghost of a smile flashed across Kirill's mouth. "Were you seen?"

"Don't think so. I've been as careful as I can. I was following you, I lost you a few times, like you just seem to take random directions sometimes, but I was able to find your tracks in the snow, or maybe I saw you moving off in the distance. Once, I lost you completely and I just kept walking, and by chance found you again."

Kirill nodded. "I never saw you."

"It was mainly because I was struggling to keep up! I wanted to catch up to you much sooner, but I couldn't move that fast. That's another reason I thought I might lose you – I can't walk as fast as you."

"Well, you're here now. Sadly, I don't have much to offer you. My food is at the bottom of the lake."

"You fell in?"

"Unfortunately, yes."

"Ah, that would explain why you are naked, then!"

Kirill said, "The camp is here. I do have a few items of food, if you feel you need it."

"Well," said Humair, unslinging his own small backpack, "on my way out of the prison, I did manage to grab a few items. Mainly, I got food, some knives, and I was able to pick up some cold weather gear. It's not much, but it will keep me going for a while."

"Yes, it's a shame I lost my gear. There was a lot of good stuff in it."

"Spilt milk, my man. We'll be okay! Here, have some dried fish."

Kirill took the dried fish, something that was salty but delicious. He nodded thank you and they both sat down around the fire.

Humair was in good spirits, warming his hands with the fire's heat. Kirill, on the other hand, was thinking over this new development. His escape may have been covered by Doctor Alastair digging a fake grave for him in the yard, but having another prisoner go absent on the same night was suspicious. The Bear was brutal, but he was no fool. He would know something was up. More than likely, he would exhume Kirill's "grave" to see exactly who, if anybody, was buried there.

"Good food, huh?" Humair held up another piece of dried fish. "The guards eat much better than us."

Kirill smiled. He took a bottle of water and unscrewed the lid, offering to Humair first who took a deep swill from the bottle, before Kirill had a drink himself.

With dismay, he realised The Bear was almost certainly in pursuit – there was little chance that he would trust in Kirill falling to the elements. He would want the satisfaction of seeing Kirill's dead body for himself. With Humair here now, he would have to be extra careful in hiding, and his resources were much more likely to be stretched.

"Where are you hoping to go to?" Humair asked.

"Mostly south" Kirill looked wary. "I will see."

"Okay, sounds like a plan. If we can get to any big town or city that's fine with me. I can disappear."

Kirill chewed in silence. After a while, he said to Humair, "Pass me that satchel over, will you?"

"Which one? This thing here, you mean?"

"No, the other one."

"Where? I'm not sure what you –"

Humair's right kneecap exploded. He screamed and fell into the snow, the bones in his leg sticking out. He looked up to Kirill in confusion. Next, Humair's wrist was snapped.

The Nightmare Man caught him by the throat, a trickle of burning air allowed in. One hand seized Humair's testicles, making them explode, his lower body becoming agony and fire.

The Nightmare Man loomed over him, a knife in his hand, teeth bared like a snarling wolf. "Not so funny now, is it? No, you dumb fucker. You've probably brought them right to me. But I'll leave a message for them. We'll see who wants to find me when they see what I do to you. After I cut your face off and skin you like a fucking frightened animal, you will tell everybody they better not follow me."

Humair, in shock, tried to kick away. But the Nightmare Man had him, and he was strong.

The blade sank into Humair.

11.

Karl was not an ordinary person. He had grown up in the town of Kurgan, which was not much more than a village, fairly close to the city of Chelyabinsk. Karl's father had worked in the lead mines for many years, slaving to provide for his family, and eventually dying relatively young from lead poisoning. Karl's mother died of alcohol-related illness when Karl was fifteen. From then on, it had just been Karl and his sister, Rhyza.

One day, Rhyza had complained to him about a local gang of criminals that were making life difficult for people in the town. Karl put down the *loshki* (spoon) he was using to eat his soup and nodded slowly. Four weeks later, Rhyza mentioned that the gang of criminals were all dead, all three of them had been hacked to pieces.

Rhyza said, "Oh my God, I can't believe it. They were bad people, I know. But this ... this is completely insane. Who could have done such a thing?"

Karl smiled and answered, "You're welcome, Rhyza."

Rhyza's eyes widened, her brother's small smile and flat expressionless eyes confirming her worst fears. "No, no, Karl. I ... I always knew there was something wrong with you, you were never normal. Oh my God, Karl. You're a monster. You ... are ... a *monster*."

Rhyza's face was contorted, a curious expression, tears and sobs coming out, eyes wide in terror, pain, ragged breathing. She fled, screaming. After she was gone, Karl stood and faced the mirror and practiced the look of horror his sister had shown him.

Rhyza reported him to the police. He felt a surge of anger, but he did not kill his sister. As he was taken into police custody, Karl didn't seem afraid at all, only curious as to where he was being taken. The answer was a large concrete building, each level being a single solid pre-made block, as was the building style during Soviet times. The *politsia* handcuffed him to a chair. Then they left him alone. There wasn't much in the room, a bare table in front of him, and a second smaller table near the door that had a hammer on it. If the hammer was meant to be intimidating, it was highly effective – for the first time, Karl felt a measure of fear at the prospect of being worked over by some psychopath. He had a graphic image in his mind of being left with all his joints smashed, crippled for life. Although the fear clawed up his throat outwardly, he appeared perfectly calm.

The door opened.

A very large man walked through; he had a uniform on and a cap under his arm. In one hand, he held a folder that contained photographs. This he put carefully on the table before Karl. The photographs were the people Karl had butchered.

In the big man's eyes, Karl read a merciless man. Suddenly, just going to prison seemed like a really good option now. He tried not to look at the hammer; in truth, he didn't want to remind the large man that it was there.

"Listen …" Karl began, "I'll be as helpful as I can, my friend. I know you think I had something to do with those people who got hurt, but it wasn't me, I wasn't even –"

"Cut the fucking bullshit, you crazy son of a bitch. I fucking know it was you."

Karl kept his mouth shut. This might all still be a ploy to get him to talk, so he would act cool for now, but he knew if the big man picked up the hammer, Karl would tell him anything he wanted to hear.

"Fucking crazy bastard. Shit, man, you don't even know who the fuck you're dealing with. I am The Bear. Remember that name."

Karl looked at the floor. Eventually, he asked, "What will happen to me? Will you send me to prison?"

He was convinced now that The Bear knew he was guilty. Such a man was unlikely to bluff about anything.

The Bear laughed. "I'm going to send you away alright, you fucking psycho. Only it's not what you think it is. You fucking butchered those people, I saw the bodies myself. You carved their cunts up like a fucking Christmas turkey. That fucking sure was something."

Karl met The Bear's gaze. "I don't understand."

"Dumb motherfucker! I'm recommending you for KGB training. If they like you, you're set for life. If they don't like you, you will never be the same. The KGB have a saying, 'if we visit you, we won't kill you, but when we're finished with you, you won't want to be alive.' That's some cold-blooded shit right there, isn't it? So I suggest you make a motherfucking good impression, shithead."

Karl sat up straighter in his chair. This news had taken him by surprise. And it was welcome news, a real opportunity to put his talents to good use.

The Bear looked again at the photos on the table of Karl's handiwork. He laughed. "Fucking crazy bastard!"

Now, many years later, Karl and The Bear stood in the snow in Siberia. Karl had become a highly respected officer in the FSB, formerly known as the KGB. There was an entire search team with them, as well as The Bear's nephew, Anton. They were all gathered around the arterial red form of Humair, the Nightmare Man's victim.

"Fuck, man," said The Bear. "This type of thing will make the search team reluctant to chase him. Fucking smart bastard."

Karl nodded to The Bear, and Anton saw a lot of respect between these two men. Personally, he thought Karl was a monster, with the predatory and soulless eyes of a shark. Everyone else seemed oblivious to this.

"Hadn't we better do something to help him?" Anton called out to The Bear. For a moment, it was Karl who fixed Anton with his dreadful eyes.

"What do you mean, brother?" Karl asked.

"Couldn't we get him a blanket or something … it's like minus 20 out here."

Karl approached the victim on the ground. He knelt and gently picked up a large section of skin, possibly from the man's back, holding it up like he was inspecting a T-shirt to see if it was dry yet. He draped it over the victim.

"Here, you must be cold," Karl said to the skinned man. "I've given you your skin back. This time, try to take better care of it!"

Some of the workers actually laughed. Karl was smiling at his audience. He regarded Anton for a moment, then turned back to the victim. "Only kidding. That was my little joke, friend. We will get you all the medical attention you need. I'm not a cruel person."

Two workers who had medical training went to assist the victim after Karl motioned to them. Karl moved back to stand beside The Bear.

"His work is aggressive but very, very amateurish."

"Don't make the mistake of thinking this guy's a fucking clown," said The Bear. "I called you here because he is so damned dangerous. Torturing dumb motherfuckers may not be his strong point, but he more than makes up for that, trust me."

Karl broke eye contact with The Bear. "You're right, of course. I will be careful. There will be no mistakes this time. Nightmare Man, huh? Well, I can assure you, his nightmare is only going to get worse."

12.

Two soldiers manned the checkpoint. There was little else but mounds of snow surrounding them and an icy road carving through it. Trees were gathered nearby standing tall in this inhospitable wilderness, the branches loaded with snow. The sun was strong. The snow was a bright lid of foam on an empty land.

"What are you doing on the weekend?" Max asked Jacob.

"I'll take my girlfriend out for pizza and a few beers. Just to our local   place."
"A few beers?"

"Heh! A few at first, yes. I'm not going to make it a really big night, we go to Church on Sunday mornings, so I got to be up early for that. You?"

Max poured them both a coffee from a steel thermos. "I'm meeting up with some friends in the city centre. We'll have a few drinks and play that card game *Mafia*. It's always nice to see my friends."

Their motorcycle was parked beside them. They had set up a small folding table with a radio and steel coffee mugs on it. The radio was playing the Toni Basil song.

"So what's your favourite beer?" Jacob asked.

"Like everybody I love the German beer."

"Yeah! It's not bad at all."

"But I also really love the Russian live beer. It's got a really fresh taste."

"I know what you mean. I could go for some of that right now." Jacob had a gulp of black coffee instead.

Max leaned back in his chair. "Do you know any jokes?"

"Yeah, why do girls watch porn movies?"

Max smiled. "Do they watch them?"

"Hey, it's a joke, Max. The answer is to find out if the characters get married in the end."

Max laughed. "Okay. You remember a few years ago there was that slogan for the Olympics, it went 'Stronger, Faster, Better,' right?"

"Yes."

"Okay, so this girl says to her husband, 'Honey, I want us to have sex like the Olympics.' And so the man says, 'Oh, you mean Stronger, Faster, Better?' And the girl answers, 'No! I mean once every four years!'"

They both laughed.

Jacob said, "I heard a comedian come out with a good comment. He goes, 'I don't believe in casual sex …no, every time I go to bed with a strange girl, I'm wearing a top hat and a monocle!'"

Max laughed. "That's a good one. You want another coffee, brother?"

"Yeah, why not. I'll even take a packet of that powdered milk shit as well."

"One coffee from former Soviet Russia coming right up."

Max unscrewed the silver thermos and poured them each a coffee in their tin cups, splashing some on the snow accidentally. He fished through his pocket and found some of the packets of powdered milk, tearing them open and tipping them into Jacob's coffee. He swirled the cup a few times and handed it to Jacob.

"Thanks, man." Jacob held the cup in his hands for a minute before drinking it. "You know, there's something about being out here in the cold, in this wilderness, that it really makes you appreciate even a shit cup of coffee."

Max laughed. "Yeah, about the only thing I learned in soldiering school was how to cook potatoes, but I can tell you it was one of the proudest moments of my life when I managed to cook them out here. I had to make the fire with whatever wood I could find, and then I had to melt the snow in the pot. They were the best potatoes I ever tasted."

"I hear that." Jacob put his coffee aside and began searching through his backpack, muttering to himself. "Where did I put it?"

Eventually, he found a flask with the two-headed eagle etched on it. He unscrewed it and sniffed the contents.

"Whiskey?"

"Come on, brother, we better not," said Max, offering his cup to Jacob. He took a generous splash and brought the cup back. Jacob also poured some whiskey for himself before tightening the lid, an operation he performed as carefully as if the flask was full of liquid gold. This time, he put the flask in the inner lining of his jacket where it would be in easy reach.

Suddenly, the Nightmare Man was there. Max and Jacob fell off their seats, scrambling for their rifles.

"Shit!" said Max, struggling with the gun.

The Nightmare Man had camouflaged himself and crawled across the snow, making his progress while the two soldiers were distracted talking to each other. Now he stood, and as Max tried to bring his rifle around to bear, Kirill knocked him unconscious with one punch.

Jacob was shoved backwards in a spray of snow, trying to unsling his gun, but he suddenly found that he was staring down the barrel of Max's rifle, now in the Nightmare Man's hands. Kirill handled the gun like an expert.

One shot …

… and the radio exploded. Kirill took Jacob's rifle away from him, packing it onto the motorcycle. With everything Jacob had been told about the Nightmare Man, he expected to die, awaiting his death sitting in the snow with a wretched look on his face, but incredibly, the Nightmare Man asked him, "Will someone be along soon to help you?"

Jacob stammered, "Uh … yeah, when I don't radio in, they will send a patrol out to find us. Within an hour."

"Okay." Kirill started the motorbike and drove off. Jacob watched him go for a moment and then went to Max to wake him up.

13.

Kirill wandered through the snow. The motor bike had run out of fuel a day ago. So he continued on foot. He had no food. He was now starving and cold. The vicious wind snapped at his clothing. The first stages of frostbite gripped his face. The two rifles he had taken from the soldiers were slung over his back. In reality, he doubted he would be able to use them at all if he needed to, because his hands could barely move. He could barely think straight. Not long later, he dropped both the rifles in the snow without even realising it.

Staggering through the cold, his mental state only became more confused. Once, he thought he saw a man following him, a man who was dressed only in rags but didn't seem to feel the cold. This man had a relentless way of moving, slow but driven. He staggered and fell down a snow-covered hill, tumbling down, landing brutally at the bottom. Kirill would have sworn that such a fall would kill a man, or at least incapacitate him, yet the stranger got up as if nothing happened. Convinced that this was just a hallucination, Kirill kept moving.

Eventually, he came to a small shed, a gift from God in these circumstances. He opened the door and went inside. There was little of any use inside, but at least he was out of the cold. He locked the door, looking for another way of securing it. There was none.

He felt a vague sense of unease about the pursuer he had seen in the snow before, but he still believed that what he had seen was impossible. He made a small bed out of an old tarp and went to sleep. Part of him knew he should stay awake a while longer, but he was truly exhausted. He should try to get warmer – if he didn't, he might not wake up again. But sleep took him.

Sometime during the night, Kirill thought he heard someone banging on the door of the shed but he was still much too tired to do anything about it. The noise didn't last long anyway, and Kirill fell asleep again immediately.

14.

Sunlight. The room was cold, but the wind had eased up. The shed had a small window. Kirill sat up and looked outside. There was snow everywhere. His eyes widened when he saw there was a farmhouse nearby. How had he missed that? He had definitely been confused yesterday, and yet … Uncomfortably, he realised he had dropped most of his possessions. He had little choice but to search the farmhouse and hope to acquire new equipment there. Otherwise, he would not last another night in this environment.

Kirill opened the door and stepped outside. The sunlight was surprisingly bright, making him shield his eyes with his arm. His eyes stung. The snow was deep and crunched beneath his boots with each step. He was about halfway to the house when he became aware of someone nearby.

Kirill turned and faced a young man who watched him impassively. He was cradling a hunting rifle. His expression was of interest and amusement. A crucifix shone for a moment around his neck.

Kirill looked calm, but he discreetly searched his environment for anyone else. There appeared to be only this young man.

"*Privet*, friend," said the young man. "How may I help you?"

Kirill kept his hands open in a friendly gesture, clearly showing he was not a threat. "I'm on my way to Chelyabinsk. I was part of a group. We were homeless, relying on the generosity of the church and any good Christians we could find. Any help you could offer me would be much appreciated, brother."

The young man nodded, thoughtful. "Sure, I'll see what I can do."

He motioned for Kirill to follow and then began walking to the house. Kirill followed about five metres behind. He saw it would be impossible to overpower this man now – he had too much ground to cover and too much deep snow to get through first, but he would almost certainly have an opportunity later.

Inside the house, an old woman was making soup over a stove.

The young man called to her, "Babushka! We've got company."

The old woman regarded Kirill with interest. The young man said to Kirill, "I'm Sasha. This is my grandmother. Well, we should have some soup ready if you would like to join us?"

"Yes, please," said Kirill. He took a seat when it was offered to him around a small table.

Sasha set the rifle down against the wall and sat opposite Kirill. He was smiling, probably glad to have some company in what appeared to be a very remote location. The table would prove a difficult obstacle for Kirill to overcome, and he still felt weak from his trek across the snow. He would need to wait before taking the rifle.

He would not leave without it.

"So where did you come from?" asked Sasha.

"I've been on the road a long time. Kind of a round trip. I'd like to visit my family in Chelyabinsk. It's been a while since I've seen them."

"Ah, Chelyabinsk. I have family there but haven't been able to see them for a while. Power lines are down, see. So we've got no communication with them."

"How're the roads going towards the city?"

Sasha considered the question for a moment. "The roads are fine. But any time I've travelled there, I was always turned back by roadblocks and soldiers. I'm not really sure what's going on."

Babushka placed some buttered bread on the table along with a glass of cold water and some black coffee. She said to Kirill, "Please eat! You need your strength."

Kirill nodded and picked up the coffee. His head was spinning. It occurred to him then just how weak he truly was. He needed rest and rehydration. The water was gone in two gulps. Babushka got him another one, and another after that.

Sasha said, "You know, I could take you to Chelyabinsk. I have a car that is reliable … most of the time. Maybe things are better now."

"That would be a big help." Kirill's vision was black, he felt incredibly weak yet he showed no outward signs of this.

Babushka placed some fresh meat on a plate and put it on the kitchen floor. A dog came into the room; it was medium-sized with black and white fur, and it had startlingly human blue eyes.

Sasha laughed to see the dog. "Malchik! Good boy!"

The dog was friendly natured and greeted Kirill as if it had always known him. Then it went to eat from the plate on the floor.

Kirill's vision was clearing. He chose to eat some bread. He still had a feeling of being disconnected from reality. If he could get some food down, he knew he would feel better.

"I think you need some rest, my friend," Sasha told him. "We have a spare bedroom. Once you have recovered, then I will drive you to Chelyabinsk. I'll be interested myself to see what is going on there. You don't mind some company, do you?"

Kirill glanced to the rifle resting against the wall and back to Sasha.

"Sure," he said simply.

15.

The road was in terrible condition. Sasha drove at high speed, seemingly oblivious to the potholes and broken road surface. Outside, there were miles of snow and trees. Very rarely did they see a house.

Kirill sat in the passenger seat gripping the armrest. He had on a new shirt, something that Babushka had insisted he take. Thanks to her, he was now well fed and comfortable. He even had new socks. On the backseat of the car was a small backpack with some basic supplies for him. Kirill had also insisted they bring the rifle.

"Well, we're almost there," said Sasha. "Chelyabinsk should just be a few more …"

His voice trailed off. There was a roadblock up ahead. Manned by soldiers. He stopped the car.

"Ah, shit," said Sasha. "Looks like we're not going any further."

"Approach them," said Kirill.

Sasha studied him for a moment and then drove slowly towards the soldiers. There were two of them, dressed in white winter tactical gear and ski masks. They held machine guns in a way that suggested they were experts.

"No fucking way! That's Spetsnaz!" said Sasha, referring to Russia's elite special forces. These were soldiers who were authorised to open fire on a crowd if it served the interests of Mother Russia, or they were just in pursuit of a criminal. Many a threat had been eliminated by them, and there were also some very dangerous criminals who had simply disappeared thanks to the intervention of Spetsnaz. It was customary that when you saw a Spetsnaz soldier on the street in Russia, you shut up, lowered your eyes, and got out of there as quickly as you could.

Sasha was struggling to turn the car around. Kirill placed a hand on his arm. "Hold it."

To Sasha's shock, Kirill was getting out of the car. "Hey! You don't want to go out there."

The two Spetsnaz soldiers watched Kirill calmly. They were obviously in control here. As Kirill walked closer and it became clear he did not intend to stop, they brought their guns up. Now he had their attention. They spread out, watching not only Kirill but Sasha as well, slowly closing in on Kirill.

The Nightmare Man held his hands up, indicating he was not armed. As the soldiers got closer to Kirill, they stopped. They lowered their guns. Incredibly, they stood to attention and saluted Kirill. He saluted them back. Then the soldiers removed their masks and embraced Kirill as a brother, shaking his hand and smiling.

"Good to see you, Captain!" said one of the soldiers.

"My brother," said Kirill to the soldier. "I need to get into the city."

"That could be difficult, sir. The way ahead is blocked; there's a wall around the city."

"A wall around the whole city? Are you fucking playing with me?"

The soldier laughed. "No, sir. After the meteor storm, the city went into shutdown. We were given orders that no one was to go into the city and no one was allowed to leave. I can't even tell you what the hell's going on in there."

"I see. A meteor storm, hey? I guess I have a lot of news to catch up on. Okay, good to see you. I need to keep moving."

"Of course, sir." The soldiers bowed respectfully and stood aside.

Kirill got back into the car. Sasha's eyes were wide. "You're the fucking Captain of Spetsnaz?!"

Kirill regarded him for a moment. "Relax, kid. You're safe with me. Now, I know I would not have gotten this far without you. I owe you. I am definitely going into that city. I don't know what's in there, but I'll do what it takes to find my brother. If you want to, you may accompany me. I will let you decide."

Kirill waited, patient.

Sasha breathed out. "Okay, let's do it. Let's go to Chelyabinsk."

PART 2

DOM 3

The Chelyabinsk meteor was a superbolide caused by a near-Earth asteroid that entered Earth's atmosphere over Russia on 15 February 2013 at about 09:20 YEKT (03:20 UTC), with a speed of 19.16 ± 0.15 kilometres per second (60,000–69,000 km/h or 40,000–42,900 mph). It quickly became a brilliant superbolide meteor over the southern Ural region. The light from the meteor was brighter than the Sun, up to 100 km away. It was observed over a wide area of the region and in neighbouring republics. Some eyewitnesses also felt intense heat from the fireball.

On account of its high velocity and shallow angle of atmospheric entry, the object exploded in an airburst over Chelyabinsk Oblast, at a height of around 29.7 km (18.4 miles, 97,400 feet). The explosion generated a bright flash, producing a hot cloud of dust and gas that penetrated to 26.2 km, and many surviving small fragmentary meteorites, as well as a large shock wave. The bulk of the object's energy was absorbed by the atmosphere, with a total kinetic energy before atmospheric impact equivalent to approximately 500 kilotons of TNT (about 1.8 PJ), 20-30 times more energy than what was released from the atomic bomb detonated at Hiroshima.

The object was undetected before its atmospheric entry, in part because its radiant was close to the Sun. Its explosion created panic among local residents, and about 1,500 people were injured seriously enough to seek medical treatment.

-from Wikipedia

It was nighttime. The Bear and his party were camped in a natural trench, protected from the wind and cold. A series of campfires kept them warm and also enabled them to melt snow for water and cook some simple rations. Some of the men had managed to trap a few small animals, setting them up proudly on spits above the fires. They passed around flasks of vodka.

Karl watched quietly, sitting apart from the group. His two bodyguards were like wolves nearby, alert but relaxed.

Karl offered Anton bread. "Have some, friend."

"No, I don't want any."

In truth, Anton was ravenous, the trek through the snow and helping to set up camp had exhausted him, but he did not want to be indebted to Karl.

Karl shrugged and went back to his food. His men watched Anton, amused.

"Hey, nephew," The Bear clapped Anton on the shoulder, "you need to eat something. Have some of this."

Anton took the dried fish that was offered him. It was salty and chewy and delicious as hell. He opened his water canteen and had some of the icy water with it. Then he remembered he had a packet of *ikra* he had kept with him from the prison. He took it out of his jacket pocket. Still cold. He had some trouble getting the packet open, his hands frozen and less functional despite him wearing two pairs of gloves, but he eventually was able to tip the orange fish eggs out onto a piece of bread with butter. He savored the taste for a moment, feeling his energy return. It was the best he had felt all day.

Looking about him, he appreciated the wilderness they were in. He had spent so much of his youth indoors, in front of a computer, in a classroom, and most recently being a guest at a prison, that he had never taken the time to enjoy the amazing country he lived in. The sky was azure with dusk's fading amber hue soaking into it. The snow was firm beneath him, unforgiving. He realised how grateful he was to have his jacket then. Given the choice between his warm jacket or a million dollars, he would choose the jacket every time.

He watched as The Bear made his rounds, checking on each of the men, making sure each man had adequate provisions and was ready to bed down for the night. The hunters had their rifles out, checking they had survived the trek intact and were in good order.

There were three guards on watch, each one leaning over the lip of the trench, a rifle pointed at the wilderness, all facing different directions. The plan was for each man to spend one hour guarding the camp. Anton wondered if he would have to take a turn. Although military service was compulsory for Russian males, Anton had never learned to fire a gun; his mother had helped him dodge the army by finding a doctor that swore Anton's lungs were too bad for him to ever join the military. He had been grateful at the time, convinced that his talents were meant for another road in life, but now he wished he had at least some basic survival skills and experience with firearms.

He decided then that he would get too cold during the night. The jacket was keeping him warm now, but the night would only grow colder. The other men all had campfires before them. He could try to join them, but he wanted to try and get his own campfire going. There was a mound of damp firewood nearby that had been gathered from the trees. There was also moss which could function as kindling to get the larger pieces of wood burning.

Gathering up some sticks, he felt self-conscious, aware that Karl was watching him, aware that he was truly out of his element. He returned to his seat which was nothing more than compacted snow, crouching down and setting up his campfire. The moss, at least, was dry; it was spongy and springy in his fingers. He lay this at the base, building a latticework of sticks over the top. Later, he would add some bigger pieces, once the wood was burning properly. He was proud of the wood structure, which supported itself without falling down. His only experience with campfires as what he could remember from TV shows.

Then he had a problem; he had no way of lighting the fire. He felt a rush of embarrassment, looking about him for something to get the fire going. Searching about him, he saw the only option was to go and ask someone else if he could take a lit piece of wood from their fire and use that to ignite the little structure he had built. The closest person to him was Karl. Carefully, he looked over to the KGB agent. Karl held up a silver lighter, amused. He had been watching everything.

Mercifully, The Bear arrived.

"Ah, I see you are making a fire. That is good. You just need to get it lit somehow."

"Yeah, about that …"

The Bear offered him a cheap disposable lighter. Anton took it from The Bear's giant hand and felt a surge of gratitude, thankful that he didn't have to go and speak to Karl.

"Thank you," he said, trying to bring the lighter to life. The lighter sparked a few times before it would light, the flame fragile, caged in his hands. He held it to the moss, its soft texture accepting the flame. The campfire burned with a low fire.

"I never leave home without half a dozen cheap lighters," said The Bear. "They are so useful."

Anton watched with some satisfaction as the flames spread from the moss to the smaller sticks.

"Is there anything else you take with you, survival stuff I mean?"

"Yes, there are a few things." The Bear extracted a bulky pocketknife from a pouch on his belt. "Something to cut with. I also carry strong cord, and a flask. Those are the basics. You can remember it this way; you need combustion, a cutter, cord, a container, and you need to find cover, something that will protect you from the weather. As long as you have those elements, you can't go too far wrong."

"Hey, thanks, I will remember that."

"Not a problem, my young friend." The Bear crouched beside him.

Anton smiled at the campfire for a moment.

"What time will we leave tomorrow?"

"Dawn. We'll have a light breakfast and hit the road. We've got everyone we can looking for Kirill, but I'm really hoping to get a grip on him first."

Anton added some wood to the fire. "You're not playing games. You really hate this guy."

"He ended up in my care for a reason, don't forget."

Anton was about to pursue the matter further when one of the men set to guard the camp suddenly called out, "Halt!"

Anton's blood froze. He couldn't move. His heart leapt into his throat. The fear was a crippling thing; it always had been. He struggled to turn his neck towards the guard who had shouted.

The guard was pointing his rifle over the trench, aiming at someone Anton couldn't see. The Bear suddenly stood up, scanning left to right, growling. Anton watched fearfully, hating himself, wishing The Bear would protect him. The Bear's eyes narrowed, his teeth bared.

"Surrounded! Everyone, pick up a gun."

The men all scrambled for their weapons, splashing through the snow, safety catches fumbled away and guns loaded. Karl looked up with what seemed to be mild interest, slowly unbuckling his jacket and removing a handgun, checking it with calm efficiency and then getting to his feet. His two men actually seemed delighted at the prospect of there being trouble.

The guard who had called out for the trespassers to halt did so again, then fired. The noise was terrifying to Anton's ears, and above all, real. Several more shots rang out, making him flinch each time. Anton was petrified to the spot, sitting with his knees to his chest. He heard the guard call out, "It isn't working! They must have body armour on! I shot that guy in the chest and he just got up again."

"Fuck, same here," another guard yelled.

The men were all leaning over the trench now, guns pointed into the night. Everyone except Anton, that is. The camp was protected on all sides.

The Bear roared, "Fire!" blazing away over the trench.

Anton saw the troops firing into the night, knowing he should do something to help, but only able to sink further into his spot. The shooting intensified, becoming closer together, presumably because the strangers had almost reached them and the men were beginning to panic.

"They won't fucking stay down!" roared The Bear.

16.

They were inside the city. The wall had been just over two metres at its lowest point, so Kirill had placed his jacket over the razor wire and they had scrambled over. Now they moved through the streets, once familiar to both of them, but now it was like they were on an alien planet. Nothing moved. Cars sat empty in the road. Apartment buildings showed no sign of life. They couldn't even hear distant traffic. It was like the city was deserted.

"What do you think happened?" asked Sasha. "Where is everyone?"

"I have no idea. Maybe some kind of plague did this. Maybe after the meteor storm, there was an evacuation and everybody left."

"Hey, if either of those things is the case, then we probably shouldn't be here."

Kirill held the hunting rifle in front of him as he walked. "You could be right, kid."

They walked through a quiet intersection and to the left of them a man sat in the road with his back to them.

"Let's ask this guy what's going on." Sasha began walking towards the stranger.

"Wait," said Kirill. "There's something wrong with him."

Sasha froze and then nodded in agreement. He had a lot of trust in Kirill's abilities.

The man on the street turned to see them and slowly stood up. He looked like a homeless person and wasn't even suitably dressed for the cold weather.

"Excuse me, sir," Kirill asked him. "We'd like to ask you what's happened to the city."

As the man approached, it became clear this was no ordinary person. He had dried blood from a wound on his neck that had covered his shirt, making it black. His eyes were disturbing, a bright white fixed in an intense stare.

"Shit, he isn't right ..." said Sasha.

As the man got closer, he changed from a relaxed gait to suddenly launching into motion, running at Kirill. The Nightmare Man used the rifle to fend him off, shouting, "Stay back! I don't want to shoot you!"

The man seized the rifle with astonishing force. Kirill found he could not shake free. Instead, he was able to bring the rifle to bear at the man's chest. The shot was loud.

There was a hole through the man's chest, and yet it didn't even slow him down. He was leaning forward savagely, trying to bite Kirill.

Kirill spun around to avoid the teeth, the strange man refusing to let go of the gun. Quickly loading another round, Kirill fired again, this time destroying the man's left hip. Still, he didn't react. He was entirely focused on attacking Kirill.

Another round tore through the man's left shoulder. This finally made him let go of the gun, but he still surged forward immediately, only to be caught in the jaw with the stock of the rifle. The man's jaw was clearly shattered, having also become detached from his face, but it only slowed him down for a moment. He seized hold of the gun again.

"Fuck you," said the Nightmare Man and shot him through the head. The top of the man's head disappeared. He fell immediately, but was still clutching the gun in a death grip. Kirill stood on the man's chest, trying to yank the gun away, "Give it back, bastard!"

All around, the apartments were suddenly turning to life. Sasha could see people, similar to the strange man, hitting the windows, trying to break out. A few more of these strange people staggered around a corner, instantly focusing on Sasha and Kirill.

"Kirill, man, we gotta leave."

Kirill was still trying to retrieve the gun. "I've seen this before. I was out in the snow and I thought I was hallucinating. I saw one of them follow me, he fell and he shouldn't have lived, but he got up again as if nothing happened. It looks like these people are all over the city."

"We need to get away. There's more of them coming. Shit, they're fucking everywhere!"

"Remain calm. I need this gun. It's our best chance to survive."

"There isn't time!"

The urgency in Sasha's voice caught his attention. Kirill looked up to see they were almost completely surrounded, and as these strange people got closer, they seemed to speed up, running towards them.

"Fuck! Alright, let's go that way."

They ran, closely pursued by the horde. The streets were deserted, but their pursuers were howling at them, a sound which seemed to wake up and draw more people to the gathering crowd.

"This is fucked, man!" said Sasha.

"We need to get off the street. And find some way of defending ourselves."

"The apartments have got steel doors out front. No way we're getting inside. Not before these people fucking get us."

"You're right. Is there something else, some other way we can escape them?"

Sasha pointed. "A fire escape over there. It will take us up and over that building."

"Let's do it."

They were on the fire escape, taking the steps three at a time and launching themselves upwards. Kirill looked back as the first of the horde reached the steps. They were congested, clashing with each other in their desperation to reach their prey. That would buy them some time.

"Keep moving," Kirill said. "We've got to outrun them."

He had a good look at the faces of the people chasing them. They all had a crazed look in their eyes, teeth bared. Behind them moved a larger crowd of much slower people, less aggressive than the group that was now climbing the fire escape.

Kirill kicked the closest pursuer back, the man flying back into the crowd and making those behind him stumble and fall on the stairs. In their desperate attempt to scramble to their feet, they obstructed each other, giving Kirill some much-needed time. He fled up the stairs to the top of the building where Sasha waited.

"This way," said Sasha. "There's a walkway made out of ladders that will take us across the street. Someone uses this place to keep off the streets."

Kirill saw the walkway Sasha intended to use. It was literally three ladders bound together to form one very long ladder that stretched to a rooftop next door.

"It doesn't look safe …"

Behind them, the first of the horde emerged from the stairs. They screamed their aggression and charged at Sasha and Kirill.

"Then again," said Kirill, and they made their way onto the ladders, walking at first but then crawling when it became obvious that falling was a real risk. It was a long way down.

The horde reached the edge of the rooftop, some of the people screaming in rage and frustration and falling off the edge onto the street. Some of the other ones regarded the ladder walkway and scrambled onto it. Its awkward shape meant that they also slipped and fell.

On the other side, Kirill and Sasha watched.

"I think we're safe," said Sasha, out of breath. Kirill watched calmly. When the creatures fell onto the street, they didn't move at all … as if they had hit their head. If anything else was injured, they just got right back up again and kept moving. There were now at least twenty smashed bodies on street level.

"Alright, I'm pretty sure they can't follow us, but we still shouldn't stay here."

They got up and crept along the rooftop. There was a stairway leading down into the dark building below.

17.

Inside the apartment block, Kirill and Sasha crept along a dark corridor. The doors to each apartment were more like bank vaults – made of solid steel – but it was the case in Russia that although there wasn't a lot of violent crime, theft and burglary were common. They were ready to run for the relative safety of the rooftop at the slightest hint of danger, but the building remained quiet. Eventually, they found an apartment with the door left open. They ran inside, Kirill doing a security sweep before bolting the door.

Kirill stood on the balcony and observed the street. He was armed with the only weapon he could find – a kitchen knife. There was no electricity, but the water still worked. Sasha was running some tap water through a filter, as he knew from experience the water in Chelyabinsk was not safe to drink.

Sasha joined Kirill to look out on the street below. "So what the hell are they?"

"Good question. From what we've seen, there seems to be two kinds of them. Those that ran after us, and were falling off the building –"

"And the slow ones like from Dawn of the Dead."

"What's that?"

Sasha smiled. "A zombie movie! You do watch movies, right?"

Kirill looked blank.

"Oh, that's right, you're Spetsnaz. You don't have any hobbies or interests at all, do you? You just train all the time and live to serve Mother Russia, am I right?"

Kirill did laugh at that. It was the first time Sasha had seen him laugh.

"I see you've read the propaganda! Well, I do have some interests outside of my work. So tell me, what do we know about these things?"

"Zombies, man."

"Alright, zombies, then. What have we learned?"

Sasha thought for a moment. "The slow ones are a lot less aggressive. But it seems like there's more of them."

"Yes. And both kinds have extremely limited intelligence, and no sense of self-preservation. On the rooftop, those things were so angry they literally didn't mind falling to their deaths. They just wanted to kill us."

"Yeah, maybe that's something we can use against them, somehow."

Kirill nodded. "Another thing is that they are incredibly strong. That one that grabbed the rifle – I'm sure I broke his arms. But he still wouldn't let go."

"You shot him in the head."

"Yes, that seems to be the way to stop them. I noticed the ones that fell from the rooftop didn't get up if they hit their head on the ground. If they get injured anywhere else, it doesn't seem to matter. They just ignore it and keep on chasing you."

"What do you think they do when they catch someone?"

Kirill turned from the street. "Some of the zombies had bite wounds on them, and also looked like they had been torn open. Maybe this disease or virus or whatever it is gets spread by bites."

"Yes, that's how it usually worked in the movies."

"Okay, so we have a basic idea of what we're dealing with. We can't afford to make any assumptions, however. There may be another type of zombie out there. And they are not the only thing we need to worry about."

"What could be worse than a city full of zombies?" Sasha asked.

"For a start, whoever built that walkway between the two buildings. Someone else is obviously surviving here. Even worse, it seems like someone has covered all this up – the Spetsnaz men outside the city are there for a reason."

"You're sure they would tell you everything?"

"They would not lie to me. If they knew what was happening in the city, they would have told me. Someone has managed to keep all this quiet. Have you heard anything at all about a thing like this?"

Sasha shook his head. "No, never."

"Well, I'm sure I saw one of those zombies in Siberia. This thing may not be contained here. And who knows how many other places this outbreak is affecting."

Sasha lowered his eyes. "I'm going to check if there's any food here."

18.

The lounge room was lit by candles.

"Here's all the food I could find, man." Sasha offered Kirill a plate of caviar and biscuits. "*Ikra* and biscuits. Not bad at all. I even found a bottle of vodka to go with it. This is almost like old times; the electricity is out for the night and I'm in Chelyabinsk with my cousin. Would you like some vodka?"

"No, I don't drink."

"More for me then. How long do you want to stay here?"

"We are safer moving at night. Harder for them to see us. I want to get to the city centre. My brother has an apartment there. And if there is any major group alive, that's probably where they'll be."

"Have you seen any other people since we got here?"

"No," Kirill took a biscuit with caviar on it, "but I have seen evidence of them. Someone is using the rooftops to avoid the zombies. I've seen a few of those bridges around. I have no idea if these people will mean trouble for us or not."

Sasha finished what he was eating "Did you find any more weapons?"

"Just knives." He regarded Sasha for a moment. "If those zombies bite you, do you want me just to end it for you? I mean, I can stab you in the head."

Sasha looked shocked. "I … I don't want to end up like one of them. Shit, those things are horrible. Alright … if I get bitten … let's just talk about it then, okay? I don't want to be one of those things, but I want to be sure first that the bite is actually what's causing all this. So don't just go killing me, okay?"

"I understand. But if they overwhelm you and are tearing you to pieces, I'll kill you then."

"Wow. You're not just cold-blooded, you have liquid nitrogen for blood."

Kirill smiled. "In that situation, I would be doing you a favour."

"Sure, sure. You're all heart. I hope I don't have to extend the same kindness to you."

19.

2 years ago …

"Vivisection has long been a hobby of mine." Karl pulled his long sleeved gloves on. He was amused at his apprentice's discomfort, although Karl's eyes showed no emotion.

The apprentice couldn't hold Karl's gaze for long. Instead, he looked at some of the jars on the shelves around the stone room. They seemed to contain various body parts preserved in fluid. There was the occasional severed head or outstretched hand, but mostly the specimens seemed to be internal organs. There were also some old textbooks on anatomy and surgery. They appeared to be well worn. On a stainless steel table, saws and blades were laid out, all within easy reach of Karl. The cutting implements were well used but cared for.

The apprentice was extremely uncomfortable now, staring at the body on the table between him and Karl, and then looking away and swallowing thickly. "I didn't think it would be like this."

"Hey, it's amazing what you can get used to." Karl held up a knife that looked like it would be appropriate for gutting a fish, appraising it in the glare of the chamber's solitary bare globe. "Say, for example, it was your job to cut people's heads off every day. Why, pretty soon the sight of blood wouldn't bother you. Pretty soon, you could cut parts off a body and not feel much of anything, really."

Karl gently patted the shoulder of the body on the table.

The apprentice looked again to the steel table of instruments, curious despite himself. The tools were not quite professional; they were more something that an enthusiastic layman would acquire rather than a trained surgeon. Still, everything must have had its purpose.

"Oh, don't feel worried." Karl read the concern in his apprentice and grinned broadly, shark-like. "This woman was charged with sedition. She was planning to overthrow Mother Russia. She had traitorous intentions towards us. Ungrateful. Uncaring. When we cut her, we might find the source of her evil nature. I'm guessing it will be her black heart!"

The apprentice could barely face Karl now, but he turned back when Karl asked him, "Do you have any questions before we begin?"

"Yeah," said the apprentice, "why does she still have to be alive while we do this?"

On the table, the woman lay with her eyes wide open, tears flooding out, breathing rapidly at two hundred breaths a minute, sweat sliding down her naked skin. She had been paralysed with medications, the type of drugs that would normally be used to temporarily paralyse a patient for surgery, and that would under ordinary circumstances be combined with drugs that would block the pain of being operated upon. The medication that was normally used to block pain had been left out. She was awake, fully aware of Karl's intentions towards her. She saw everything.

Karl grabbed a shiny mirror on a moveable, jointed steel arm. He carefully pointed it so the woman would be able to see everything.

"Not so funny now, is it, Arita?"

The KGB agent laughed.

20.

He stumbled down the tunnel, almost no light to find his way. Clutching his jacket, he stepped over the railway tracks, almost falling, catching himself before he could. The gravel crunched loudly, no other sound. The tunnel was empty, just him trying to get away from the open hatch. It led into darkness. From the darkness came a howl. It sounded almost human. The man straightened, alarmed at the proximity of this sound. For a moment, he seemed to weigh up the choice of running away or going back and trying to seal the hatch that lay open. His breathing was quick and desperate. Lurching forward, he managed to catch himself on the open hatch before he could fall over. There, he rested for a moment before summoning himself, putting forth an almost heroic effort to get the hatch closed, leaning his entire effort into swinging it shut.

The man looked up at the caged globe above the heavy steel door, illuminating his face. He looked similar to Kirill. This man was known as Biter.

Struggling with the lock, he realised it wouldn't roll closed – there was no way to lock the door. He smashed the valve several times as he might somehow get it closed, but nothing worked.

Slowly, he began to back away, clutching his side, watching the door which could spring open at any moment. Then he staggered up the tunnel.

21.

Standing on the parade ground with the other soldiers, Kirill was wearing his basic trooper uniform. The wind snapped at his clothes, the cold fresh. They all stood in a line, these men who had passed the Special Forces training and joined the elite ranks of Spetsnaz, the most formidable fighting force in the world.

The Sergeant moved down the ranks, shaking each man's hand in turn, and pinning a Spetsnaz badge to his chest. No words were necessary.

Kirill stood in the cold sun. He felt alive, a quiet sense of victory in the air. This was just step one, the beginning of his career, but everything else would spring from this day.

22.

Kirill and Sasha stood on the balcony, watching the streets below. The street was packed with zombies, some of them vicious, snapping at the air and growling. Most of the ghouls, however, were slow and awkward, turning to face each new sound, driven by primitive instinct. Individually, these zombies were nowhere near as dangerous as the faster more powerful zombies, but in such large numbers, that barely mattered.

"It's as if they know we are here," said Sasha. "There's no way we can run through them. Not with them packed together like that."

"No, we can't go down there. Not now. But maybe there'll be an opportunity later."

Kirill had tucked a large knife into his belt, one of the few weapons he had been able to find.

"The way they move ..." Sasha studied them, "It's like they follow sound. Maybe there's something in that. Maybe if we can create a distraction somehow, we can divert them away from us."

"The problem is more will come. I haven't seen any survivors yet, so it is best we assume the whole city has been taken over; everyone is a zombie, or else an enemy. Anyone who has survived this has to be dangerous. If we make noise in this area, it may very well draw zombies away from us. But it will also alert the other zombies in the city and make them come here."

"Well, you're the badass special forces soldier. What do we do?"

Kirill looked away from the window. "Right now, we wait. We study our enemy and see how they behave. Maybe they will forget about us and wander off. For all we know, they may lay down and go to sleep at nightfall. There are some bottles of alcohol here. We can make some Molotov cocktails out of them and –"

"Alcohol, you say? That gives us something to do while we are waiting!"

"You can drink if you wish, I need to be at a hundred percent in case our situation changes."

"Oh, come on! Have a drink with me."

"I don't drink."

"You're like the poster boy for Spetsnaz, aren't you?"

"What do you mean by that?"

"Like, all the propaganda says that Spetsnaz guys don't have any hobbies or anything else they do, except serve Mother Russia. That's what you're like."

Kirill didn't respond, so Sasha asked him, "What do you do in your spare time?"
"I like to train. I like being on the shooting range."

"I mean for fun. Leisure activities, man. What do you do for enjoyment?"

"Training is enjoyment for me."

"Alright, look, I don't want to sit here drinking alone." Sasha poured two glasses of vodka. "So will you have a drink with me?"

"I'll leave it, thanks."

"But you just got out of prison. Surely that's reason enough to celebrate?"

The Nightmare Man considered for a moment. "Give me a glass."

Half a bottle later, Sasha and Kirill were sitting down on the couches. Sasha was smoking a cigarette, something which Kirill refused to do.

"You know, we didn't always get it right," said Kirill.

"Huh? What didn't you get right?"

"The missions … sometimes we had bad information. Or we didn't use the information we had correctly. That cost us a lot. It really did."

"Oh, I'm sorry …"

"Like, there was one time we had to kick this terrorist's door down and kill everyone inside. We were waiting just outside his door; our hearts were jumping out of our bodies, each one of us was full of adrenalin. Then intelligence got the word that it was the wrong house, they'd made a mistake, and we were standing outside the house of an innocent family. They screamed at us on the radio, 'No! No! No!' but we were so hyped up that what we heard was 'Go! Go! Go!' so we kicked the doors in and killed everyone inside. We didn't even realise until the end."

Sasha sat still with the cigarette burning in his hand, unnoticed.

"There was also another time, another mission. We had intelligence that a terrorist group was hiding in a building. There was no one else in the building, just the bad guys. Nearby was a house with a family in it. We had the authorisation to drop a bomb on the terrorist's house. The problem is that the person in charge was reading the map wrong. See, the way he was looking at it, he thought the family's house was the terrorist's house."

After long moments, Sasha asked, "So what happened?

"I argued with him. I showed him how to look at the map correctly. He wouldn't back down. My men spoke to me and asked me what we were going to do. I said, 'We have to follow orders. We're Spetsnaz, that's what we do.' So I made the call, I gave the pilots the go-ahead and the bomb was dropped, killing everyone in the house. Afterwards, we watched it all on the satellite image; we saw a group of terrorists run out from the other building. We'd made a mistake, and killed another innocent family."

Kirill didn't look quite so tough right then. The alcohol had made him say far more than he would have said under normal circumstances, but that didn't seem to register with him yet.

Sasha said nothing, just went to the window to see if there had been any change to the crowd of zombies downstairs.

23.

Andre was the new Tsar of Chelyabinsk. He was a former Russian Mafia man, quite adept at solving problems, whether they are to intimidate a local businessman into giving a percentage of their income to Andre's boss or on occasion even doing work on behalf of the Russian government. In the aftermath of the zombie outbreak in Chelyabinsk, Andre had an opportunity to rise to power, as he saw this time not as many saw it; an apocalypse, the end times, but instead as something of a dream come true for a man of his qualities. If not for his association with the Russian Mafia, he would have spent his life in jail, or worse. But with the dead walking and attacking the living, Andre shone in this new world.

He set up his base in the military academy in Chel, once known as "Tank School," sharing this building with gangsters who were resourceful enough to survive in a city besieged by zombies. This building had been an academy for soldiers who were fighting in tanks, until it was eventually closed down and turned into a laser tag facility. It was occasionally used as the set for horror movies. In the foyer, Andre had set up a gathering place for his people, a base of operations where he could speak to his people in real time. The other rooms were full of supplies such as food taken from nearby supermarkets and stolen guns.

In the centre of the reception were six zombies chained together. They were imprisoned in a rough enclosure of steel girders imbedded in the floor. The zombies strained against each other, trying to move in opposite directions, helpless where they were, but serving as an excellent reminder that Andre could feed a disobedient person to them at any time. He liked that idea a lot.

Besides, the six zombies were Andre's former bosses.

"We got a problem, boss," Masha said. She was one of the finest gangsters Andre had, beautiful and tall, with the half-Asian eyes that were typical of people from this region, clear blue. The kit she carried was light and practical, well thought out. She had a rifle supported on one hip. She was the best shot out of all of Andre's people.

"Yeah? What's up?" Andre sat up straight. He never slouched when talking to Masha. On the floor beside Andre was a silver AK 47.

"Company. I don't know who these two men are, but one of them is a hard case. He seems like a professional to me."

"Okay, okay, what did you see?"

"I was watching them through the scope; they ran from the *zombi* and got into an apartment building. I don't think they will be going anywhere. They are totally surrounded."

"They ran from the *zombi*, so what? We do that every day."

"I forgot to mention, I was following these guys as soon as they got into the city."

Andre paused, understanding. "They got past the Spetsnaz outside. That couldn't have been easy. Okay, you're right, these two could be a problem."

Masha smiled. "What should I do?"

"Kill them – don't wait. No fucking around, just kill them from a distance. I won't take any chances with these two."

Masha nodded. "It's as good as done."

By the main entrance, the Mafia guards suddenly drew their weapons, some of them holding up poles with blades at the end. Outside, there was a swarm of *zombi*, crowding around the entrance, howling and trying to reach the humans inside. The Mafia troops were cold and professional, unalarmed by the presence of the horde as they drew back the sliding locks on the main door. At the far corners of the building, the lookouts there started making noise and causing a distraction, shouting insults at the zombies and banging against the windows. It had the desired effect; the crowd began to disperse, many of the ghouls drifting away from the front door and to the windows. When enough of them were gone, the armoured car rolled up to the front door, being allowed through. The Mafia guys at the door were well armed and covered head to toe in protective gear. They seemed to see the straggling zombies who tried to follow the car in as more of an annoyance than anything else, skewering them with their improvised spears and keeping them pinned while another troop ran forward to club the zombie down with a crowbar or similar item.

The entire exercise was well rehearsed and effective. Within moments, the few zombies who had made it inside were all expertly dispatched and dragged away from the entrance. The crowd outside who had by now realised they had been deceived now tried to converge on the open doors. The guards stabbed several of them down before retreating inside, once again blocking the heavy steel door. It was a simple enough routine which the Mafia used every time they needed to send people out on supply runs.

The doors to the armoured car opened and Mafia looters from inside emerged, each one dressed in fine clothes and the Russian *sharpka* hats, also decorated with medals. They were laughing as they brought out bottles of vodkas and jars of ikra, handing the prizes out to the other fifty or so Mafia people who were cheering in response. All in all, another successful trip.

24.

There was movement in the apartment below. Brandishing a knife, Kirill went out into the corridor. There was a lift, but he chose the cold cement steps, chipped and broken. He watched from the stairwell, listening, ready to run back to the apartment if he had to. A zombie emerged from the corridor, staggering at first, then moving faster and growling when it saw Kirill. Its arms were outstretched.

Kirill deflected its arms aside and expertly buried the knife in its head. The zombie stopped moving instantly and fell. Kirill tried pulling the knife out but it was stuck, driven into the hilt. He looked up as the door to an apartment swung open, six zombies inside. The first one was on him while he was still registering the scene and attempting to retrieve the knife. Kirill recovered quickly, driving the zombie back with his forearm and punching it in the jaw with his other hand. The punches would have been devastatingly effective on any normal man, shattering their jaw and leaving them unconscious; however, it had little effect on the ghoul. It was still reaching for him.

He shoved it back into the apartment; it fell as it collided with the other ghouls. They fixed him with their sickening eyes, moving forward. Kirill seized the heavy iron door and swung it closed. It was not locked, but it would buy him some time to get to safety.

Behind him on the stairwell, Sasha whispered, "Are you okay?"

"We move now."

Sasha moved quickly behind Kirill, taking the stairs to the lower levels. They heard the apartment door open and the zombie's claw out onto the stairwell.

"Keep moving. We can't afford to get caught."

The ground floor was dark, but there was enough light coming through the dirty windows for Kirill to see. The walls had letterboxes on them for the apartments. There were seven slumped bodies on the floor. Kirill paused for a moment, a small knife in his hands, waiting to see if the bodies would move. They didn't. He set foot on the ground floor.

Glancing nervously up the stairwell, Sasha followed. A powerful steel door led out from the apartments. Kirill pressed the release button beside it, gripping the door firmly and opening it the tiniest amount. The sun that came through blazed like a blowtorch.

"Come on, man, we got to get out of here," Sasha said.

Kirill said nothing for a moment, studying the street outside. Several zombies were spread out on the street, some of them sitting down leaning against parked cars amid old newspapers, a few more shuffling aimlessly. Kirill said, "There's zombies out there, but we should be able to move between them. When we move, stay close to me. Make as little noise as possible. We need to keep moving."

"Wait, wait, man, maybe we should just go back to the apartment. You know what happened last time we were outside."

"There're zombies coming from upstairs. We need to do this now."

The Nightmare Man was right; Sasha could hear them. The zombies that had followed them from the apartment were howling, and in response, more howls were coming from the apartments. More heavy apartment doors were pushed open. More steps gathered on the staircase.

The bodies on the floor began to growl, slowly sitting up.

Kirill was startled, ready to start killing every one of them.

Sasha was breathing rapidly, unsure what to do.

"Come on," said Kirill, flinging open the heavy steel door. The light from outside was blinding. Sasha retreated for a moment, but Kirill had seized his shirt, dragging him with shocking strength out into the street.

Several zombies paused to investigate the sound of the heavy door opening. Kirill was moving instantly, running for the main road. It would lead them to the city centre. They ran fast, fueled by adrenalin. Behind them, zombies began pouring out of the apartment building they had left.

The street was dirty. Cars were left askew in the road, sometimes with their windows smashed and trails of blood leading out. There was garbage in the road. They passed a skeleton beside a burned car, both of them blackened. There was the shell of a baby basket in the back seat. Moving around the car, Kirill avoided a reaching hand from a zombie lying on the road, turning to kick the creature in the face.

"God dammit! We need to get off the road," said Kirill.

There was a faint explosion and a chip of road burst apart beside Kirill. Sasha looked down at his own leg. It was bleeding, fierce. His eyes widened, hands going to this new wound.

"Get down!" hissed Kirill, pulling Sasha to the road and behind the car.

"What just happened?"

"Someone's shooting at us."

"I … I've been shot?"

"Yes, but I don't think it's serious. We need to get out from the open; we can use the buildings for cover and get the hell out of here."

"You mean like the apartment? We were safe there." Sasha was smiling. Blood ran through his fingers.

Kirill edged around the car and retrieved a broken side mirror from the road. He held it around the side of the car, scanning the buildings.

"Some girl is shooting at us. She's set up in a building across the road."

"Some girl wants us dead? Maybe we should talk to her, tell her were not … not like them … we're human …" Sasha was going pale.

"I don't think she wants to listen."

Suddenly, another shot rang out and a nearby car was hit. Then another car was struck. And another. On the fourth shot, the car's alarm screeched into life. The noise was enormous in the street. All the nearby zombies looked their way. The zombies that were sitting rose to their feet. Holding the small mirror, Kirill was sure he saw the shooter smile.

"Shit! Now all the zombies know we're here." Kirill kept low, seeing zombies approaching from all around them.

"Don't leave me here, man, don't leave me," Sasha said, but Kirill did exactly that, fleeing and using the cover of the cars as best he could while the zombies closed in from the surrounding streets. Some of the ghouls gave chase to Kirill, but most of them zeroed in on Sasha, as if sensing he was the vulnerable one. The sniper made several attempts to shoot Kirill, but he moved in a zigzag irregular pattern, moving from car to car so he was difficult to shoot. Bullets smashed the road around him as he ran.

Sasha realised, bitterly, that he had been a fool. With a name like the Nightmare Man, there was no way he should have had anything to do with Kirill, let alone trust him with his life. Of course, Kirill would do anything to complete his mission to find his brother. Including leaving Sasha to die.

He lay on the road, watching Kirill go. Looking frantically around him, he saw the zombies were almost on him. He used his good leg to kick away, scooting across the road breathlessly, pressing his back into the burned car, trying as best he could to hide. His breath came ragged and fast, worst now that death was near. Everywhere dark shapes loomed closer. Even through his fear, he noticed the girl in the building across the road. She had stood up now at the smashed window, obviously aware that Kirill and Sasha were little danger to her. She seemed to have the gun aimed at Sasha, and he thought it would be far more merciful if she did shoot him; it would be a much better way to go then being eaten alive by the crowd of zombies. But she seemed content just to watch events unfold, leaving Sasha to his fate as the noise of the car alarm drew even more zombies.

Sasha glanced about him desperately for a weapon of some kind. His intention was not to try and fight off the horde. He was long past believing there was any escape here. The reason he was searching for a weapon was to end his own life before the zombies reached him. There was nothing nearby that could be used to end this. He released his hands from his leg wound, letting the blood flow free.

The first of the zombies crept around the side of the car; she was an old woman, literally skin and bone, pulling herself along the car and cautious at first, but then hissing when she seemed to realise Sasha wasn't going anywhere. Now there were more ghouls to the opposite side of him, two men now, they might have been businessmen in their former lives. Sasha's head sank onto his chest, a pool of blood gathering around him. He prayed the end was quick, and that the blood loss would kill him before the zombies did.

"Fuck you, Nightmare Man."

The zombies had reached his feet now, excited that they were going to tear him apart. He heard a car in the distance, over the sound of the nearby car alarm. He didn't associate any significance with the car engine sound.

The old woman growled into his face, now just inches away. He was frozen in terror, the cords in his neck threatening to snap.

Suddenly, a car was roaring towards him, hitting some of the other cars left on the road but definitely destined to run Sasha over. This car seemed to have zombies lashed to the roof of it. He watched with interest, actually relieved that he would be run over instead of eaten alive. The car swerved moments before hitting him, smashing into the zombies instead. The driver side door opened.

"Give me your hand!" shouted Kirill. Sasha reached out, and Kirill yanked him into the car with one arm. The car was a taxi, no seat belts, the left-hand side had two destroyed zombies broken and stacked together on it. They were seat-belted into place. When the sniper started shooting, Sasha could see why; the corpses blocked the view of the sniper. Shots smashed into the zombies tied to the roof, others going wide and hitting the road. Kirill drove in a haphazard fashion, trying to be unpredictable, trying also to avoid the zombies that were now approaching. Sasha crawled to the backseat, watching as Kirill was trying to drive and keep his head down.

"Sorry I left you back there," Kirill shouted, "but we needed some way to get out. I hope you can forgive me."

Sasha clamped down on his leg wound again. Moments earlier, he had been prepared to die. Now, he was desperate to live.

"Thanks for coming back for me."

One of the front tires exploded, destroyed by a sniper shot. The car turned to the side violently, smashing into three zombies who were sent flying. They landed in the street and immediately got up again. Kirill fought for control of the car, struggling to keep from crashing. He hit another zombie who was knocked over the roof of the car before landing in the road. It was on its feet again in seconds, howling and pursuing the escaping vehicle.

"Russia's worst drivers," said Sasha. "I think I saw this on TV."

The car fishtailed around the corner, one final bullet smashing through the driver-side window. They were now, temporarily at least, away from the sniper.

"We can't go far in this thing," said Kirill "We just need to put some distance between us and the sniper. Then we can find something else to travel in."

Sasha lay back down on the floor of the car. Everything had a detached feel to it, as if he was disconnecting from reality. He remembered it was important to keep pressure on his leg and he did, fading into darkness.

25.

Less than two blocks away, Kirill crashed into another car. He had been driving on a steel rim anyway. There were zombies in the street but most of them were being drawn towards the car alarm from the car the sniper had shot. Kirill lifted Sasha from the back seat, carrying him almost effortlessly. As he got out of the car, a nearby zombie's head exploded, almost instantly followed by another. Kirill flinched, keeping his head down, understanding that the sniper was toying with him. He ran for a nearby restaurant, taking him out of the line of sight of the sniper for now.

It was dark inside. Kirill lay Sasha on the table. "Keep pressure on your leg, comrade. I will search for medical supplies."

Kirill moved into the nearby kitchen, scanning for enemies from the doorway as he went. Normally, this type of room clearance would be carried out with a machine gun, but all he had now was a knife. The kitchen seemed safe enough so he went inside. There were open cupboards full of dishes and shelves stacked high with food. At least they wouldn't go hungry. Nearby, he found a green first aid box. He removed it from the wall and put it on the bench. Inside, the contents were basic. He closed the lid again and returned to Sasha with the plastic first aid box.

"We need to keep the pressure on your leg, my friend." Kirill was taking fresh gauze from thin plastic packets.

"Aren't you going to try and remove the bullet like Rambo or somebody?"

"No, safer to leave it in there. If we get out of this mess, I'll take you to a doctor. In the meantime, you've got me."

Kirill took his belt off and measured Sasha's leg with it, using his knife to make a new hole for the belt buckle. He carefully moved Sasha's hands aside, quickly placing the gauze on the wound and then wrapping the belt around and pulling it tight, a crude but effective tourniquet. Kirill disappeared for a minute, rummaging around the kitchen and returning with two water bottles. He unscrewed one and gave it to Sasha.

"Thanks," Sasha took a big gulp, "but I thought it was bad to drink water when you have an injury?"

"Probably, yes. But as we will most likely be dead soon, I thought you would not like to do thirsty. Am I right?"

"I guess so."

They could see out on the street and see the zombies walking passed. The relative darkness of the restaurant meant it would be more difficult for anyone else to see in.

Two of the zombies outside were expertly shot through the head and fell in the street. Kirill ducked behind the counter, watching carefully. Where Sasha lay on the counter, he could not be seen from the street. Another zombie fell, close to the car they had used to escape the sniper. Kirill drew his knife.

He crept as quietly as he could to the main window, being careful to remain hidden from the side the shots had come from. Leaning forward slowly, he peered out onto the street.

The sniper walked boldly down the middle of the road, clearly expecting she would not be shot. She cradled the rifle like a beloved child. Any time a zombie got too close, she shot them through the face with her handgun, almost as though they were unworthy of being killed by her rifle.

She had noticed the crashed getaway car with the zombies strapped to the roof and was moving towards it. She stopped suddenly mere metres away from where Kirill lay hidden in the dark. If he had a gun, he would have made the ambush now. Instead, he had his knife brandished. He knew she was a decent shot with the rifle and an experienced killer. Better to wait for her to move a little closer to the restaurant, or better yet for her to have her back to him.

The sniper removed a compact CB radio from her jacket. "Masha here. I'm chasing two people on foot. One's wounded, badly. The other one will be slowed down by him. I'll search for a few more minutes then I'm coming home. There're zombies approaching from everywhere."

Kirill waited while she put the radio away, her jacket sleeve moving up to reveal tattoos. His eyes widened. He was almost certain they were Russian Mafia tattoos.

When the radio was back in its pocket, Kirill inhaled sharply, ready for the kill. The moment she took one more step, she was dead. Suddenly, she turned around, there was someone watching them from a nearby rooftop. Masha had the rifle ready in an instant, but the young man was already fleeing. Masha began approaching the building that the observer had fled from, walking away from the restaurant. Kirill sank back into the shadows, still able to see her.

She stood in the street as zombies shuffled forward, drawn toward the car alarm that still sounded. Masha scanned the buildings as if trying to work out where Kirill and Sasha were hiding. She used the scope of her gun to scan the windows of the surrounding buildings but found nothing. Eventually, she took off her small backpack and flung open the straps. She took out a Mickcy Mouse alarm clock. She wound it, then tossed it casually in the street, very close to the restaurant where Kirill watched.

The ringing of the alarm was noisy and it drew more zombies. Masha walked away. She didn't look back.

26.

His name was Semyon. He sat on the counter beside Sasha, who was still unconscious. The Nightmare Man still had his knife drawn.

"You were lucky not to be shot," he said to Semyon. "That woman knows how to kill."

"I'm an experienced runner," said the young man. "I've grown good at hiding and avoiding danger."

"So what the hell's going on in this city?"

Semyon smiled grimly, taking a water flask from his slim backpack. "Zombies, man. I don't know what else to tell you. One day, they were just there. And everybody began dying. Only problem is, they got right back up again."

Kirill waited impatiently, expecting a thorough debriefing, when that wasn't forthcoming, he said, "Why was the woman after us? She clearly saw that we were human."

"That's the New Mafia, man. They've got loads of guns. They take new recruits sometimes. But you got to be real tough to join them."

"So nothing's changed there, at least."

"Ha! You got that right."

"Why didn't you leave?" Kirill glanced out onto the street. He had disabled the Mickey Mouse alarm clock, but there were still about ten zombies outside the restaurant.

"Couldn't. There's a wall around the city."

"So that was just there overnight? The zombies were here instantly, and so was the wall?"

Semyon thought for a moment. "I don't know if the wall was there right from the start. But it was certainly impossible to leave. I heard reports of people getting shot if they tried to leave the city. There was no internet and no radios or television working. Anything we heard was just from other people on the street."

"Are you part of a group?" Kirill asked, but Semyon laughed nervously and looked away.

"You said you were a runner. Does that mean that you transport important items? Or that you have to distract and draw the zombies away?"

"All that and more, man!"

"Okay. Do you have access to any guns?"

"They are out there; the problem is getting into people's homes to get the guns out. You practically need safecracking equipment to get into an apartment. But if you can do that, you might find a machine gun or something."

"I'm better with a gun."

"Well, I'm better on my feet. I'm going to get some supplies. There're hungry mouths to feed."

Semyon got off the counter in a fluid movement and went into the kitchen, plucking food stores from the shelves and putting them into his backpack.

Kirill checked on Sasha. He seemed to be stable, a little pale, but the bleeding was under control. The zombies on the street were reluctant to disperse; they had been drawn by the sound of the alarm clock, and it was as though they expected humans to return soon.

"Do you just run?" Kirill said quietly, but in the relative stillness of the restaurant, Semyon was able to hear him.

"That's my specialty, man. But I do a good job of climbing, too." Semyon came back with his backpack full of food items. "I set up some of those ladders, you see. Most buildings are pretty spread out, so there wasn't much point even trying to connect them. But some of them are close enough together that all they need is ladder between them. Makes running from the *zombi* a lot easier."

"I agree."

Semyon held up a packet of dried seafood. "This is a good find."

"Do you know where the Mafia are held up?"

"The New Mafia are based in the Tank Academy. You can't miss it. They have wild parties every night. The noise and all the music draws a lot of zombies so they tend to have a crowd around them. Doesn't stop them from doing what they like, though. They're doing very well through all this."

Semyon shouldered the backpack, testing the weight to make sure he wasn't overburdened.

"This restaurant still has a lot of food I could use. I'll come back here every morning at four for the next few days. If I see any sign of your sniper friend, I'll run away. Otherwise, you and me can chat some more."

Semyon walked directly to the entrance of the restaurant, tightening the straps of his backpack as he went. Incredibly, he walked out onto the street in front of the zombies and was too fast to be caught. He ducked under their reaching hands and was away, fleetly disappearing with the zombies staggering clumsily after him. The Nightmare Man watched him go.

27.

Kirill rode the motorcycle with Sasha on the back. He had "acquired" the Harley Davidson from the carpark at Megapolis.

Sasha's leg was bandaged with rags, a loose end flapping in the wind. The wound was treated four times a day by Kirill cleaning it with water and then pouring sugar into it. This simple battlefield technique was almost as effective as antibiotic therapy in keeping a gunshot wound from becoming infected. Here on the outskirts of Chel, there were no zombies around; he could believe for a moment that he was back home visiting his brother and everything was peaceful. He slowed as he saw the wall in the distance. A two-metre high concrete perimeter with razor wire on it encircling the city. It was enough to break the illusion. Kirill brought the motorcycle to a stop.

"I'll need to change your wound again," said Kirill. "We can stop here."

"Do you think the sniper will find us here?"

"I think we're safe enough." Kirill kept his eyes forward, scanning.

"Why the hell was she even shooting at us? Didn't she know we were human? My God, I can't believe she wanted to kill us."

Kirill steered around a wheelbarrow full of picks and shovels. "I did see her after I fixed up your leg and we were holed up in that restaurant. That sniper girl was following us. She came very close to where we were hiding, to the point I was going to kill her with a knife, but she moved away. She didn't see me, but I saw her. I saw she had some tattoos. Pretty sure she's Russian Mafia."

"Great, just what we need. It's not enough that we're stuck in a city full of zombies, we've now got a sniper from the Russian Mafia after us."

"I don't think she's the only one."

Sasha sat up straighter. "But they're fighting the zombies, too. Surely a lot of the Mafia people must have been killed by the zombies, along with just about everyone else."

"The Mafia are professional killers. They're probably enjoying this whole thing. For all we know, the Mafia could be stronger than ever."

Nearby were work machines, earthmovers and the like, lying dormant for some project that would probably never be finished. Pickaxes and shovels were left beside mounds of gravel. There was gear for workmen, including safety vests and hard hats. No sign of any workers.

Kirill brought the motorcycle in slowly, ready to speed off at the first sign of trouble. There were a number of places for people to prepare an ambush, including a tin shack with the door hanging on one hinge and some of the machines provided excellent cover. He weaved around piles of rubble, driving in generous circles. There were barrels of chemicals and fuel for the machines, warning labels declaring that the contents were flammable.

There were also crates of explosives.

Kirill's eyes lit up when he saw them. He was fascinated by all types of weapons. After driving through the entire work site and being satisfied that no one was waiting to harm them, Kirill brought the bike to a halt beside the explosives. Sasha carefully disembarked the motorcycle, limping with his bad leg. They had stopped at one of the frequent pharmacies all around Chelyabinsk and acquired some painkillers, which he needed now. He swung his backpack off his shoulder and onto one of the barrels, flipping open the compartment with the medications in it. He broke the painkillers from their packet with a satisfying crack and took two of them with some water from a bottle. He offered it to Kirill who also had a drink before giving the bottle back.

He found a crowbar and had the crates open a few minutes later.

"Intact," Kirill said.

"That's a hell of a lot of bombs," said Sasha.

"They're not bombs yet. The detonators are missing." He scanned the yard again. "The detonators are probably in that shack."

"And if they are not there, you can make them yourself, right?"

Kirill smiled. "Yes."

Kirill looked to the explosives and then back to the city. He had a plan.

28.

Semyon dropped to the floor of the Megapolis entertainment centre and rolled, quickly getting to his feet, and ran. Eyes wide, looking back behind him, desperate. The zombies were in close pursuit, two of them, running after him with wild surging movements, shrieking and snapping at the air, hands clutching to reach him. They were filled with insane rage …

Megapolis had formerly been a popular venue in Chelyabinsk, complete with cinemas, video games, a bowling alley, and an impressive range of restaurants. The restaurants held a variety of food from around the world such as Japanese sushi, Brazilian meat on swords, Chinese food, and German beer. It had been popular among young people but also old people as well, who could enjoy a quiet meal at one of the huge restaurants and then watch some of the traditional Russian dancing taking place before they retired for the evening, while the younger people would stay on to enjoy the nightlife as the restaurants swiftly turned into nightclubs. Many Russian venues served shisha, which was a flavoured tobacco-smoking device that filtered the smoke through water. These devices looked a lot like the devices that people used to smoke marijuana, but in the restaurants, it was only ever flavoured tobacco that was served.

An endearing feature of Russian cuisine was that they openly borrowed from many other cultures, choosing an impressive variety of food from around the world and serving that in many restaurants, so that a restaurant which claimed to serve Japanese food would actually do an excellent job of providing Italian food as well. These restaurants were typically served by student waiters and waitresses, mostly looking bored out of their brains. They tended to work long hours, too, which didn't help matters. In fact, it was common for many people to work a twelve-hour day and for many shops and restaurants to be open quite late at night.

Now the restaurants stood empty.

Semyon ran through the silent halls. His pursuers were always just behind him. Semyon called out as he ran, only making the fast zombies more eager to catch him. He tried changing direction suddenly to slow down his pursuers and create some much-needed space. It worked; they weren't as agile as him, but they were relentless, so that any advantage he seized, they worked to get back again. He pulled a potted plant down behind him. The two zombies smashed into it, both of them colliding and spilling over onto the floor. They were on their feet in seconds, giving chase again. Both of them were clearly injured but showed no sign of feeling pain.

His feet pounded the floor. He could not remain ahead of them indefinitely. Rounding a corner, he saw the cinemas nearby. The two zombies growled and ran at him. Semyon was sprinting again. He was running towards a row of video game machines, the lights still on. One of them was the claw game, the tray beneath the claw being stacked full of little stuffed toys. The bright yellow panels reminded Semyon of many nights he had had here as a customer, before the zombie apocalypse, when he had been a young student himself, enjoying his life. The image of the claw game brought back the memory of better times. Suddenly, the claw game tilted forward violently, crashing face down on the floor.

Semyon didn't slow down. Instead, he dived over the fallen machine, sailing through the air, then rolling onto the floor to absorb the impact of landing, and then sliding away across the floor on his back. He slid across the floor until he was stopped gently by the next corner. He now faced the way he had come, watching the two zombies try to navigate the fallen obstacle.

In their eagerness to reach Semyon, both zombies tripped and fell over the machine, landing heavily on the floor. Before they could get to their feet again to continue chasing Semyon, the Nightmare Man stepped out from behind one of the machines. He was carrying a steel baseball bat. It was him who had tipped over the machine.

Two hard swings and both zombies were unconscious, their jaws broken.

Semyon brought his knees to his chest and then sprang into the air in a hip-hop move, landing on his feet in one lithe movement. He was not out of breath at all as he approached Kirill.

"Man," said Semyon, "I sure hope your crazy plan works."

Kirill did not take his eye off the two fallen zombies.

29.

In a small shop, the front door creaked open. A zombie turned around to face the sound, moving slowly towards it. There was food supplies scattered on the floor, dried fish, chocolate bars. There were stacks of bottled water that hadn't been looted yet.

Without hesitation, Kirill leapt up to the zombie and smashed it in the jaw with his baseball bat. It fell and was motionless. Semyon followed him in a silent crouch, scanning for danger.

Three more zombies stood up from behind the counter. Kirill was on them almost instantly, kicking the first one in the chest so it was sent flying backwards into the other two zombies. They struggled on the floor to rise again, but Kirill was already attacking them with the bat; it sounded like they were made of wood as they were struck.

In moments, the store was still again. Semyon gathered supplies, filling his backpack with much-needed food items. He separated some of the water bottles from their plastic container and slid them into the backpack.

Kirill held the bat high, ready to strike again, always expecting danger.

Ten minutes later, they were in one of the cinemas back at Megapolis. It was full of people. They were refugees from the city outside, now huddled together in the huge dark building.

Sasha approached them, limping on his bad leg, offering them black coffee.

"How'd you guys go?"

"Hey, we made it back in one piece," said Semyon, taking a cup. Kirill held the steel bat leaning comfortably on his shoulder and took the second coffee. He was very aware of his surroundings, studying the rows of people who were trying to sleep or else get some food, which was always in short supply here, no matter how many runs Semyon made. It was dangerous to go outside, and not only because of the zombies; the New Mafia were an ever-present threat.

Kirill looked about the cinema again. There was a young priest who was preparing for the next sermon. Many people had already gathered around to hear him speak. The water supplies they had were all blessed by him. The front row was full of children and some parents of those children still lucky enough to have parents. More people filled the rows behind them. Lastly, they were joined by the older crowd.

"Do you go to church?" Sasha asked Kirill.

Kirill studied him for a moment. "I don't have much time for it. Don't take me the wrong way, I think Christianity helps a lot. I know many guys who carry a Bible with them when we go on a mission. And I do own a crucifix."

Sasha laughed. "Yeah, okay, but I mean do you ever set foot inside a church?"

"Like this one, you mean?"

"Okay, so church is not for you."

Kirill thought for a moment. "I get that Christianity is good for holding the community together. It gives our people a common identity. But it's not for me."

"Yes, it does help a lot. It helps to know there's a higher meaning to all this, that in the end we're all going somewhere better."

Kirill said nothing to this, so Sasha continued, "There's also a lot of nice ideas in Christianity, like forgiving your enemy."

"No disrespect, comrade, but you can't forgive a zombie. If you try to make friends with it, then it will kill you. Do you think I should try to forgive that woman who was shooting at us?"

"Well, we don't know the full reason she was shooting at us, do we? It may well be the case that one day we're working with her. I mean, we're all in this together, after all." Kirill wasn't buying it, so Sasha looked over to where the priest was almost ready to begin his sermon. "When the dead are coming back to hunt us, a little forgiveness among ourselves could really go a long way."

The priest came over to them, hands held out.

"Ah, Semyon, great to see you." The priest clapped Semyon's shoulders. He said to the Nightmare Man, "My friend, my name is Father Gorodetsky. We all really appreciate your help here. Semyon says a lot of good things about you."

"Not a problem, Father Gorodetsky, my name is Kirill. It looks like your help is needed here. I'll keep on helping Semyon with his supply runs. It would be a good idea to tell your people not to set foot outside."

Gorodetsky nodded deeply. "I understand. The dead returning to life is a terrifying thing."

"It's not just them. As I understand, the Mafia are still active. They have snipers. They don't seem to care who they shoot."

"I don't think these people would venture outside again unless they had to, but I will make sure they get the message. Kirill, would you be willing to say a few words to the congregation?"

"No disrespect, Father, but I think that's a bad idea. I do my work from the shadows."

"Please, Kirill, these people need hope in such a dark time. A few words from you could really mean a lot to them."

Everyone was now looking at them. Sasha and Semyon were also curious to see how Kirill would react.

Kirill did not raise his voice but everyone heard him. "Sisters and brothers. I know how terrible things look right now. But we will endure. We will overcome this. Always remember, we are Russians."

Silence. Kirill nodded once. He had given many brief speeches like this before leading men to war. Long, glorious speeches were for men who never fought. Kirill turned away; he had many things to do. Someone began clapping. It quickly caught on.

As Kirill turned to face the audience, people were standing up and applauding him. Cheering.

Semyon laughed as he clapped, "Yeah! We are Russians!"

A chant began, "Kirill! Kirill!"

A woman clapping her hands together said to him, "Thank you for saving us, Kirill! We need your help."

Sasha said to him quietly, smiling. "You're a hit, man."

Kirill looked back to him. "This is all just work to me. I'm here to do a job, nothing more."

30.

The horde crossed the frozen river. There were thousands of zombies in the dark, moving together, drawn by the sound of music playing from the building. Snow crunched beneath their feet. Most of the streetlights were out. But the building was lit with its own light; there were disco light effects, green beams, camera flashes, spotlights. The New Mafia made no attempt to disguise their presence. In fact, quite the opposite. They announced to the city they were there, loud and more glorified than ever.

The party at the New Mafia building had already brought hundreds of zombies to surround the building, trying to break into its concrete walls. Now they were joined by a much larger horde, sweeping across the city, and adding to the ranks of the zombies gathered waiting, desperate to gain entry and attack the New Mafia.

31.

Semyon distributed food among the survivors in the cinema. He tried to make sure everybody got some dried seafood, which kept well and was nutritious, but it was mainly the staples of cooked rice that was keeping them going.

Sasha stood with Kirill. "So when do we put your crazy plan into action?"

"Tonight," Kirill said simply.

They walked out of the cinema out into the foyer. Some of the arcade machines were still working, glowing in the otherwise poorly lit foyer. There was an enormous plastic box that had once held popcorn, long since drained.

A life-sized statue was used to advertise a new film, which none of them would probably ever see. Kirill stopped and studied the figure; he had walked past it a hundred times, but now it caught his attention.

The movie was this winter's hit horror comedy, Grim Teenager 3. The statue used to advertise the movie was a teenager wearing a grey hoodie, the hood up to make him reminiscent of the grim reaper, the letters "ANGST" written across the chest in silver. He had grey baggy trousers on. He gripped a huge scythe and held it threateningly before him, slightly crouched as if ready for combat. His eyes glared and were striking because they had no irises, just pupils.

The writing on the cardboard underneath the grim teenager read "Grim Teenager III" made to look as if it was written in fresh blood, and below that was the tagline, "No one knew what he was angry about."

Kirill studied the baby-like face of the statue again.

"I wonder if that scythe is real."

"Probably is," said Sasha cheerfully. "Russia is a country with low health and safety standards!"

Kirill crossed the foyer and stood before the Grim Teenager. He lifted the scythe from the statue's hands, testing its weight. He turned to face Sasha with the curved blade before him, as if ready to cut his enemies down.

"Now that's an omen if I ever saw one," said Sasha.

32.

Andre sat in the main entrance of the former tank school. The Mafia were spread out before him, partying to loud music, drinking vodka, taking drugs. They wore some of the most expensive and fashionable clothes available in Russia, including items from the *Gum* clothing store in Moscow, where a T-shirt could cost a thousand dollars. Several of the hunters were drunk and swinging from the open doors of the armoured car, laughing and spilling champagne. They wore gold jewelry as well, usually in the form of crosses from the Orthodox church, the main religion in Russia. The girls were wearing their best makeup, dazzling, eyes bright, lips red. A crate of *champonskoe* was opened and champagne glasses were filled for everyone.

Andre shook one bottle of champagne and opened it so it drenched the six zombies in the metal enclosure in the centre of the room. He laughed a lot at his former bosses. They became more aggressive, shouting and trying to reach him. Each one of the Mafia bosses had a bullet through their heart.

Andre looked from the six Mafia bosses to the silver six-shooter tucked into his belt.

"Six bullets, six bosses," he said.

Masha ran up to him, holding her rifle. "The hard case is back! He's strapped bombs to the *zombi*!"

Andre was still processing what he had just heard when there was an explosion outside. One of the zombies in the horde just beyond the door had exploded, blasting another twenty zombies into pieces. Andre ran to the window, Masha beside him. She was talking and explaining, but Andre quickly realised what was happening; there were a number of zombies with exploding vests strapped to them. These vests had a flashing light on them and a small antenna, which made him think that someone was detonating them from nearby. And really, there was only one person that could be.

"Shoot those zombies!" Andre called out, the music suddenly switching off. "The ones in the vests! He's trying to use them to blast the gates open."

Dazed with the effects of drugs and alcohol, some of his people were slow to act, but they moved to the windows and started shooting. The first problem was that the handful of zombies who were wearing explosives were well protected by the ordinary zombies in front of them. These had to be cleared away first, which the Mafia did in a barrage of gunfire. When the explosive zombies were revealed, they found their next problems; these zombies were also wearing protective head gear. This was a mixture of hard hats and crash helmets, but it did the job of deflecting a number of bullets before each one of these zombies could be brought down.

Masha quickly fired at the approaching zombies, destroying one zombie bomb with each round she fired, but she realised she wasn't shooting them fast enough. Andre also fired into the advancing zombies, some of his bullets going wild, others smashing into the faces of these zombies and bringing them down. Another explosion went off. Then another. Some of the bomb wearing zombies had been destroyed in the blasts, as well as ordinary zombies, but there were still more zombies approaching due to the noise that was created.

Many of the Mafia bullets were shot wide, missing due to their drunken state. Masha and Andre continued to thin the crowd, carefully selecting the zombie bombs and making each shot count. Just as it looked as though they had destroyed all the zombies approaching the front door, an explosion rocked the building – one of the walls to their right had been blasted in by the closest explosion yet.

With horror, Andre realised the breach was too big to block up. It was now only a matter of time before the rest of the zombies started pouring through. And they seemed to be approaching from every direction, drawn by the noise.

Andre physically pulled some of his people away from the windows to defend the breach in the wall. Four Mafia people stood blazing into the crowd, gunning down the advancing zombies, cheering into the night. When the gun smoke cleared, a lone zombie staggered up to the hole ripped into the building, it was ripped to pieces by bullets but saved by the kevlar helmet it was wearing. A lone Mafioso aimed his shotgun at this zombie. Masha saw what was happening and tried to shout at this man to stop, but he took his shot, hitting the zombie in the face but the spread from the shotgun also detonated the zombie's explosive vest, killing all four of the mafia guards in the resulting explosion.

The hole in the building was now even wider, smoking rubble spilt across the floor. The Mafia folk were now beginning to lose their nerve, suddenly aware they could lose control of the building. The armoured personnel carrier was still an option. Andre ordered the drivers in there, then pushed Masha in as well.

She turned back to Andre. "What about you?"

Andre paused for a moment, considering fleeing in the safety of the armoured vehicle, but he was, after all, Mafia, and he would not turn his back on his people.

"Go!" he told Masha. "Get some distance from here. Draw them away if you can. Or at least try to thin their numbers. If we fall, then make sure you live."

She looked like she was going to cry for a moment then she closed the door.

Andre assessed the scene; the zombies still hadn't gotten into the building yet, but there were huge numbers outside. His people were still gunning them down, but they would eventually run low on ammunition. It would be just a matter of time before the zombies reached them, and then their only option would be to fight a retreating battle, probably retreating to the second floor and defending the staircase for as long as they could. After that, who knew? Exhaustion would eventually take its toll. There could even be a number of reserve explosive zombies, which the Nightmare Man had kept back to mop up any survivors that weren't killed in the first wave. And if one of those exploding zombies detonated on the staircase while Andre and his people were defending it? Why, his glorious reign would come to a sudden end.

33.

The Nightmare Man moved through the dark. From what he could tell, his plan was working. The zombies with explosive vests were mixed in well with the horde of regular zombies and had advanced upon the Tank Academy. The New Mafia were shooting at the crowd of zombies; somehow, they had realised the danger. He saw the explosion that broke the building open, allowing the crowd of zombies in. While the New Mafia were focused there, he would be able to approach the building unscathed, or at least that was the plan. As he watched, most of the crowd of zombies seemed to be focusing on the hole in the building, sensing that at last they could reach the people inside.

More bombs went off. These were ineffectual, serving only to destroy twenty or so zombies in the crowd each time a zombie exploded. The zombies who were not destroyed outright in the explosions continued to crawl relentlessly forward, still determined to reach the New Mafia inside.

His first order of business would be to find a gun. He knew he would be much more effective once he held a firearm. Kirill made his way towards the battle on foot. The night was cold. He felt alive.

Nearby, a sports car with two of the New Mafia inside noticed Kirill. They leaned out their windows with machine guns, firing wildly at him.

Kirill ran for the only cover he had – straight for the zombies. Ducking under clawing hands, he merged with the crowd. Bullets chewed through the crowd of rotting meat, smashing the zombies apart, splintering bone. Zombies shook and fell all around him, being ripped apart by the bullets meant for him.

Kirill suddenly faced a zombie with an explosive vest on. Jackpot.

He stood and swung his scythe into the zombie's neck, piercing it through its neck and straight into its rotted torso. It growled as black blood fountained out of it. In one mighty movement, Kirill turned and swung the scythe with the zombie on it, the growling zombie was flung off the blade and hurled at the sports car. It flew through the air and the two Mafia guys fired at it. Just before it could connect with the car, it exploded, splashing the front of the car with flames. Kirill expected them to abandon the vehicle, but instead, they both jumped inside, spinning the wheels in the snow and then plowing into the crowd.

Zombies were smashed down before the flaming vehicle. It smashed through them, seeking out Kirill, but the crowd of zombies made it difficult to see. The flames quickly went out from a combination of the car's speed and zombies bouncing off the front of the car.

Turning on a wet mound of smashed and broken zombies, the car came to a halt. There stood Kirill with the scythe in his hands.

The driver, a bald Mafia man, grinned and revved the car.

Kirill brought the axe scythe back as if ready to strike an opponent, but he was half a block away. He swung the scythe forward and let it fly. It swooped through the air in a nightmare arc, flashing as it caught the moonlight, sweeping toward the car. A stray zombie got in its path and the flying scythe exploded through it in a wet splash without slowing down, as if destroying a cloth bag full of water balloons filled with black ink.

Baldie ducked as the scythe burst through the windshield, but the passenger was not so lucky. He was impaled in his seat. He gasped once and was dead.

Baldie looked out to Kirill who stood weaponless. "Motherfucker! You are dead now!" Revving the engine, snow splashing high as the car began to fishtail, he was a caged bear waiting to be released.

"Better check your passenger," Kirill said calmly.

Baldie's eyes widened. He snapped around to see the passenger, who came to life as a zombie, clawing and scratching to reach him. Baldie screamed in defiance, trying to keep his former friend at bay. The car spun in a circle, smashing zombies into the air, and suddenly stopped. All around, zombies closed in.

The Nightmare Man turned and ran for the New Mafia building where the battle was heating up.

34.

Andre gathered his people in the foyer. Smoke from bullets and exploding zombies filtered by. His people were sobering up, the drugs and alcohol leaving their systems as they once again became what he needed them to be: killing machines. Good. He would need all the help he could get. It seemed like every zombie in the city was converging on their headquarters.

Andre checked his AK 47. Still plenty of bullets. They had a reprieve, for now. It wouldn't last.

Beside him, a racing car driver dressed head to toe in a yellow and red flame design held a scoped .44 Magnum in her hands. This was the Rose Maniac, his best driver.

"Rose, you're better in a car than stuck in here. Cut a path through the zombies. See if there is any way of taking their attention somewhere else. Remember, someone out there is looking for us. Someone dangerous enough to strap bombs to zombies. So ... take care of yourself."

Rose nodded. "I'll find us a way out, boss. Then I'm going to find whoever's responsible, chain him to my car, and drag him around the city until there's nothing left."

Andre smiled. "Good girl."

The Rose Maniac marched in a straight line toward her car, a red beauty of a machine. She almost casually decapitated three zombies that got in her way, the huge handgun roaring. She dived behind the wheel with the ease of a cat. A moment before she could close the door behind her, a fast zombie appeared, seizing her wrist.

She shot it once through the heart and it let go, but now it was the Rose Maniac seizing hold of the zombie's arm. The engine roared to life. She dragged the zombie around in a tight circle. Cheering erupted from the Mafia. The zombie growled in what sounded like anguish. This is what it would look like when she caught the Nightmare Man. Then she allowed the flailing zombie to fall beneath the wheels. It was cut in half in seconds, trying to crawl away. The Rose Maniac pretended to drive away, as if giving mercy to the zombie who dragged its ropey intestines behind it. Instead, she flung the car in reverse, screeching across the floor, crushing its skull as it looked up.

The Mafia cheered as she zoomed into the night, scattering zombies into the air. When they crashed into the ground, they kept on crawling forward if their heads had not been crushed.

Andre grinned. Somehow, he felt better about this whole thing. He motioned to his people to the back of the room. More zombies were pouring in through two breaches in the walls. The front door was also left open.

Andre took a tarpaulin aside, revealing two giant anti-aircraft guns. They were facing more or less the approaching zombie crowd.

"This game is far from over," he told his people. Two Mafia gangsters moved to the guns, ready to defend their home.

35.

Kirill was inside. He had crept onto the second floor when a series of three zombies had exploded, taking attention away from him. He had seen the Mafia guys fighting on the ground floor. No way he could take them, not without a gun. The zombies would keep them occupied. For a while. But he thought these Mafia guys were good, maybe good enough to stop the whole damn zombie horde.

Not if he could help it. He would need to move fast. To somehow kill as many of the Mafia as possible. If he couldn't, then they would always be a threat, not just to him, but to the survivors holed up in Megapolis. This had to end tonight.

An explosion burst through the floor dangerously close to him. He was knocked off his feet, watching the third floor come down and crush the spot before him. His way was blocked. Rolling to his feet, he was already looking for another way round. Gunfire everywhere. This was a war. He was home.

People approaching. He leapt behind a corner, a split second before he could be discovered. The Nightmare Man's blood ran cold. He couldn't believe it. The Bear. He had followed him from the prison. Beside him was a much smaller man who seemed out of the place.

The Bear spoke to his companion, "You stay on this floor, nephew. Things are going to get exciting very fucking quickly. Fucking crazy bastards!"

The Bear seemed to be enjoying himself. That wouldn't last long if Kirill had anything to do with it. There were other guards from the prison, too, that Kirill recognised. They followed The Bear loyally. Staying to the shadows, Kirill followed the group.

Eventually, there was another explosion which distracted them long enough for Kirill to seize the one The Bear had called "nephew." He could well prove to be a valuable prize.

Kirill seized Anton and withdrew as the smoke and dust collided around them. He heard The Bear call out "Anton!" but they were already twenty metres away, and Kirill carried Anton easily as he ran still further.

He ran up to the third floor before he put Anton down.

Anton stared at him in disbelief. "You're the Nightmare Man!"

"I am."

"A lot of people want you dead."

"That never changes." Kirill drew his knife, giving Anton a good look at the shiny blade. It was the same knife he had used to skin Humair alive. "I have questions."

36.

The sign read simply:

The Russian Dentist

In the white room was a woman strapped to a dentist's chair. The Dentist was a woman named Olga, a thickset woman that looked like she could carry a telephone pole. A white dentist mask hid her face. Black locks spilled out from her paper cap. She held a whining drill in her hands as she loomed over her patient, who fought against their bonds. The patient's mouth was held open with blocks and her head was fixed in place to the chair, but her body writhed as if she might somehow be able to escape The Dentist's drill.

"Andre has questions," said The Dentist. "Don't worry, I can still understand what you say. Let's start with where your group is hiding."

Just before she could drill into her patient's teeth, the door was kicked in.

Senior KGB Agent Karl was there, the door having been burst in by one his assistants.

Karl smiled broadly as he stepped into the room, Olga straightening up and standing away from her patient, still holding the drill. Karl's assistant moved to block the door, gun drawn.

"I like your style," said Karl. "Everyone has a fear of the dentist. And something tells me that your patients fear you, especially. Well, as much as I would love to study your work, I will have to stop you here. Because I have questions of my own."

Olga's eyes were wide above her mask.

Karl picked up an instrument from a steel tray. It had a hook on it.

"A man named Kirill. Is he here?"

Olga didn't answer, so Karl said, "You might know him as the Nightmare Man. Trust me, if you've made him angry, you'll know why he is called that. Last chance; please tell me where I can find him."

"Kind sir, I genuinely do not know," said Olga as Karl got closer. "All I do is work for Andre. If he needs someone to talk, I make it happen."

"Hmm, yes, I understand. But you seem like the kind of person that people would like to talk to. I bet you hear a lot of things. And if your boss has an enemy, or a new friend, then I am certain you would know about it."

"Please, don't hurt me," said Olga, sobbing and falling to her knees.

Karl studied her for long moments. Then he looked at the hook in his hand.

37.

VOLGOGRAD, 2013

The newspaper on the table showed images of the bombing of the Volgograd train station. There was a photo of a babushka crying. This terrorist attack left the entire nation shaken. Humair sucked on his cigarette and held up the newspaper, appraising the bomb scene.

They were in hiding now; it seemed that all of Russia was looking for them. But they had made their statement loud and clear. All that was left was to reach the border and make their way through Kazakhstan to their contact person. Then they would live out the rest of their days in luxury.

Arita came out of the kitchen carrying food on a tray. She was doting and adoring of Humair, the man who had been an important part in setting the bombs at the train station.

She placed the tray of food on the table beside him, careful not to obscure Humair's view of the newspaper photo, which he was still looking at and smiling over.

The window smashed. A small smoking device landed on the floor. Humair regarded it with surprise while he sipped his coffee. It suddenly exploded into blinding light and Humair was on the floor, deafened and blind.

He could not see the front door burst in with a battering ram or the four Spetsnaz soldiers charge through. He did not see Arita punched unconscious and then handcuffed and dragged outside, while the special forces soldiers checked every room.

A Spetsnaz soldier in a white ski mask and uniform stomped on Humair's face, leaving him unconscious.

Later, when Humair was downstairs with his jaw broken and his hands cuffed behind him, he saw Arita again. She was being shoved into a van. Normal citizens on the street ducked their heads and got away as fast as they could. No one stopped to film the Spetsnaz or interfered – everyone knew the Spetsnaz were not to be messed with.

Humair caught a glimpse of two men in the van. They were the hated FSB, formerly known as the KGB.

One of the men was Karl.

Humair himself would be interrogated thoroughly. At first, he would try to hold out, but within moments, he would sing like a bird and tell everything he knew. The Spetsnaz men holding him punched him in the chest twice, breaking his ribs, and he was thrown into a waiting car.

When the car was gone, the Captain of the Spetsnaz men spoke to his troops. "That's a good start. The KGB will make those two give up everything. Then we're going to find every person who was involved in the bombing. And we're going to kill their wives, their parents, their children, anyone who had anything at all to do with them. We'll exterminate their entire bloodlines. Hell, we'll even kill their green grocer."

The other three Spetsnaz laughed.

The Captain slung his machine gun around his neck. This was the Nightmare Man.

38.

Anton was handcuffed to the frame of a car. Terrified, he shrank from the zombie who was also cuffed to the car, snapping and biting to reach him, restrained so it was just out of reach.

The Bear called out, "Anton! I'm coming to get you."

Anton was gagged, but his eyes were wide. He was trying to say something as The Bear ran towards him.

The zombie tried to reach The Bear now. He regarded it without fear.

"Crazy bastard," he said, and stabbed it in the head. It stopped moving and fell limp, held up by the handcuffs keeping it attached to the car.

The Bear ripped Anton's gag out of his mouth, "Anton, I'm glad to see you –"

"The zombie! We have to get away!"

The Bear looked back at the zombie, and in a moment, he saw two things. First, he saw the zombie was wearing an explosive vest. Second, he saw on the level above the Nightmare Man, holding a detonator.

The Bear's eyes widened. "You fucking crazy bas –"

The zombie exploded, enveloping The Bear in flame and throwing him on fire thirty metres through the air. He smashed through a wall, part of the roof falling in on him. The floor above leaned in precariously, causing a safe to slide across the floor and down through the newly created hole and land on The Bear's head with a metallic clunk.

The Bear was still.

Anton was still alive, having been largely shielded from the blast by his uncle.

The Nightmare Man was with him in a moment, holding his knife in front of Anton's face.

"Thanks," said Kirill. "That's one less bastard to worry about. Now I just need to kill that son of a bitch Karl, and put a stop to the New Mafia. Don't worry. I'll make this quick."

He raised the knife. Anton cried out, certain the Nightmare Man meant to kill him.

Then The Bear's men were there, aiming guns at Kirill.

In one movement the Nightmare Man cut through the supporting structure that Anton was attached to. Sparks flew. Kirill grabbed Anton and moved away from the men with guns.

"Let him go!" one of the men called out.

Kirill was holding Anton as a human shield. "You have no business here, comrade. Get away or I will give your man back to you in pieces."

The men were muddled and confused, unsure how to respond. Before they could gather their wits, Kirill had run out the room with Anton. He closed the door behind them and blocked it with a vending machine, effectively barring the door to Anton's dismay, The Bear's men now following close behind.

Kirill shoved him up the stairs, pushing him towards the second floor.

Anton was terrified, but for once, he was more angry than scared. "You motherfucker! You killed my uncle! I hope they send you straight back to that little cell!"

The Nightmare Man paused on the stairs. He still had his knife in his hand. He used it to indicate the way forward.

Anton kept climbing. When they reach the second level, they could watch the battle between the New Mafia and the city of the dead from a hole in the floor. It seemed like a thousand zombies were swarming the building with the New Mafia fighting them, using guns or else close-combat weapons, ranging from swords to one man fending off the zombies by swinging a statue at them, holding the life-sized figure by the feet. The statue broke and the man wielding it picked up a poker machine instead and swung that at the approaching zombies.

"The *zombi* are everywhere now," said Kirill appraising the battlefield, "and that's scary."

Anton was shaking with fear and anger. "What do you mean? Are you scared of them?"

Kirill laughed without humor. "I'm always scared."

Anton was sure the Nightmare Man was making of fun of him, but he was still curious. "You? Afraid? But you were a Captain in Spetsnaz. You're one of the most dangerous men in the world."

"I'm the biggest fucking coward you've ever met in your life, kid. Trust me. Everything scares me. I'm frightened of my own shadow. But I embrace my fear. I hold it close. I welcome it. Fear is like a jealous wife: if you scorn her, try to deny her, then she becomes your worst enemy. But if you accept her and hold her close to you, then she becomes your best friend. That's all I do. I admit that I'm frightened, then I embrace my fear. And then the fear makes me stronger."

Anton regarded him for long moments.

"Thank you."

The Nightmare Man turned from the battle scene to face him for a second but said nothing. The battle raged on.

Then Kirill pointed the way forward with his knife and they continued down the corridor. They were heading towards the foyer of the Tank Academy. They were at a bar, bottles of alcohol everywhere.

They could see the foyer from where they were, and in particular, Kirill saw the KGB agent, Karl.

Kirill turned to Anton. "Stay here. If things get dangerous, I suggest you run away or hide. There are a lot of high-caliber people around right now."

Anton nodded grimly.

Kirill paused for a split second as he was leaving. Then he handed Anton his knife. "This may help protect you if you need it."

The Nightmare Man smiled faintly and then left him at the bar, marching towards the foyer, ready to kill Karl.

39.

Masha was in the passenger seat of the sports car. The Rose Maniac was driving. They sped down a muddy road, the car bumping over holes, the occasional zombie getting in the way and being knocked into the air like a bowling pin.

"We're going to kill this man," said the Rose Maniac. She gripped the steering wheel lightly with her red leather gloves.

"Yes, he caused it all," said Masha, checking the enormous rifle. "I want him to suffer. I'll shoot his legs off and feed him to the zombies."

The Rose Maniac said nothing. The lights of the car cast a powerful cold beam upon the road, blinding. There were two rocket launchers on the hood of the car, operated by a joystick near the gear stick. A stray zombie was walking beside the road, lit up in a wash of white light. The Rose Maniac swerved the car slightly to destroy the zombie. It went under the car with a bump and did not move again.

"What were you before all this?" asked the Rose Maniac.

Masha looked out the window and answered, "I was in IT. I helped put in a lot of the infrastructure for this region. Bringing internet to people. Putting in speed cameras on the roads. My team was behind all that. I loved that job. And then the apocalypse happened. The end of the world, as far as we know. Or maybe it's just here, and life is going on like normal everywhere else. It's hard to imagine what a normal life is now. And what about you? What were you doing before the meteorites fell?"

The Rose Maniac changed gears. "I was in the Mafia, before the meteorites."

"Really? They recruited me because I've always been good with a gun. Why did you join the Mafia?"

"I didn't have much choice. I had a psycho for a brother. Seriously. He was the only relative I had, so when I ran away from him, I guess I felt I needed someone to protect me. The Mafia was the answer. They're my family now. It seems like they always have been. I love my new brothers and sisters, I really do."

"Yes, I feel the same way. The world is hell now. All we've got is each other. I don't know why this thing happened, why the zombies came, but they are reality now. This is how our world is. We've got to do everything possible to hold onto each other. I think of the New Mafia as my family as well. I kill for them, and if necessary, I will die for them."

They passed a tenement block with candle light in a window. A person was watching them but quickly retreated. The Tank Academy was not far now.

Masha turned to face the Rose Maniac. "Thank you for helping me back there. I thought I had a good position on the roof of that shop, but then that alarm went off and starting attracting zombies from everywhere. I'm a good shot, but I couldn't have killed all of them. Thank you for saving me."

"Anytime." The Rose Maniac gave Masha's hand a squeeze. "You're my best friend. I wouldn't leave you."

Masha held up the rifle and looked through the scope to study the Tank Academy building. Then she calmly fed a shell into the breech of the gun.

"He's there, right in the foyer. I'm going to end this now. Keep the car steady." Her words were calm, almost conversational. The Rose Maniac did not respond, only kept driving the car back home.

40.

Karl arrived at the foyer. His bodyguard Misha walked beside him.

"We have an advantage over Kirill," said Karl. Misha only listened obediently. He gave the appearance of a man who was physically powerful but slow-witted; however, when his master commanded him to do something, he was very effective. Now he walked in silence and listened to Karl speak.

"You see, everyone hates Kirill. He messed up badly by attacking the Mafia, of all people." Karl gestured with his hands. "They are more against him than they are against us. He let those damned ghouls into this place. If I could speak to their leader, maybe we could combine our resources."

"I think I could arrange that."

Karl turned around. The Dentist was there.

Karl smiled. "I would appreciate the help!"

She smiled obediently.

"Anything for you."

Karl seemed jubilant. "This really is a crazy situation, isn't it? All these dead people returning to life again. You know, I have put a lot of bad people in the ground. Wicked, wicked people. It's funny to think they could be walking around again. I wonder if any of them think of me, if there's some part of their brain that remembers, that is looking for the man who reduced them to that state. What a day that would be if we were to meet again."

The Dentist said, "I would give anything to learn every single thing you could teach me, sir. So that I could put wicked people into the ground, too."

Karl slowly turned to face her. His eyes were wild. Then he laughed. "It really is a shit world, wouldn't you say? So many bad people everywhere. So much work to be done to correct that situation."

"They're everywhere, sir."

"You know, that doesn't even matter. I know there's one good person in this world, one person who's not like everyone else, and that's my sister."

"I'm sure she's a wonderful person, sir."

"She is. I haven't seen her for years, but the last time I saw her, she was in Kurgan, which isn't very far from here. It's a small town, not very interesting. But that's where I come from."

"Hold it right there," said the leader of the New Mafia. He had a gun pointed at Karl's head. The KGB officer's smile froze. Slowly, his hands came up. Misha went for a gun, but Andre growled at him, causing him to rethink his intentions.

"I'm actually really glad you're here!" said Karl.

"Really? I wouldn't be, if I was you."

"I just wanted to talk with you about working with you."

Andre pressed the gun into Karl's neck. He gripped the trigger hard, milimetres away from ending Karl's life.

"This is not a negotiation."

"Everything in life is a negotiation, my friend. I want to kill the Nightmare Man just as much as you do. More, probably. I really think we can help each other."

Andre grabbed Karl's lapel, pulling him tighter against the gun. Now Karl's smile was gone, fear in his eyes.

The Dentist said, "We can use him, boss. I believe him when he says he wants the Nightmare Man dead."

"You understand who he is, don't you? Men like him have no friends. He would torture his own mother if the state told him to. That's just the way he is."

"Guilty as charged!" Karl still had his hands up, only now they took on a quality of mock guilt, as though he had been caught eating a cookie before dinner.

"I understand who he is," said The Dentist.

"And why do you think there is any benefit to letting him live? The safest thing to do is to kill him."

The Dentist paused before answering, "That's true, but he has specialist information on the Nightmare Man. He may be able to help us catch him, or at least understand his tactics."

Karl grinned at The Dentist. "Hey, thanks!"

"How do you intend to catch the Nightmare Man?" Andre asked Karl. "He has proved to be somewhat problematic up until now."

"Well, for a start, your men have to stop attacking my guys. We should all be working together to stop him. Right now, we're divided; not only do we need to defend ourselves against the ghouls, but we also have a vicious killer running around who could strike anybody at any time."

"Is that the only insight you have? Stop killing each other?"

"I can tell you that right now we are playing into his strategy. He wants to see us distracted and divided, fighting a war on two fronts. He is meaning to frighten and demoralise us. The zombies are very good for that. You have one added advantage to doing business with me – Kirill hates me. He will willingly come out of hiding to try and kill me. You may as well use that to your advantage."

"I see," said Andre "And what're your intentions towards this guy? What are you going to do if you catch him?"

Karl's eyes lit up. "I am supposed to return him to his prison cell. I am supposed to hand him over unharmed."

Andre smiled. "I'm guessing that's not going to happen."

"No way on this earth. He has done too much damage since he got out. Killed way too many people. He is an enemy of the state. And that's where I come in. To punish someone who has harmed Russian citizens."

Andre asked, "Will you kill him?"

"We have an expression in the KGB, 'If we visit you, we won't kill you, but when we're done with you, you won't want to be alive.'"

"I like that. Sounds like the bastard will get what's coming to him. Okay, I'm going to lower my weapon now. Any bullshit, any hint of trying to harm my people, and I will just kill you. I won't talk with you a second time. Do you understand what I have said?"

"Got it," said Karl. Slowly, the gun was taken away from his face.

"You stay up here on the first floor where you are nice and visible," said Andre. "I'm going to the ground floor. As soon as Kirill approaches you, I will be there to ambush him."

Karl grinned. "Good plan!"

"Okay. Olga, are you going to be okay here?"

"I'm fine, thanks, boss," said The Dentist.

"Stay safe. Our entire fucking dream is in danger now. All of us … are in danger now."

He left them behind, going to the staircase. The lights were out so he held a thin torch into the gloom. Fleet of foot, he descended the staircase making almost no noise. Halfway down, he almost ran into two his people, a man and a woman.

"How are you doing?"

"Not bad, we're just getting some more ammunition for the guys fighting at the walls. The anti-aircraft guns are helping a lot; without them, we probably would have been overrun by now. We can do a good job of keeping the *zombi* out, but they will get the better of us, sooner rather than later."

"Keep up the good work," said Andre. "We're almost through this. Once we kill the Nightmare Man, our lives will get a lot easier. The bastard must have some kind of remote detonator; he can make zombies explode when he pushes a button."

"We found a trap before that must have been set by him. It almost took my head off, but we were able to shoot it down so it wouldn't hurt any of our people. Be careful, boss, we've never been up against a guy like this before."

"You know it. If I don't see you again, then I want you to know it's been an honour to live by your side."

The three Mafia people embraced. Then the two Mafia soldiers went up the staircase and Andre continued to the ground floor. He could see areas where his people were fighting to keep the monsters out, attacking them with swords through ruptures in the concrete walls, or shooting them when groups of zombies got through. His people were more organised now, the initial shock of the exploding zombies having worn off somewhat.

Andre kept to the walls, scanning the huge room.

"How am I going to find you, you son of a bitch?" Andre asked out loud.

"Looking for somebody?"

Andre turned. It was the Nightmare Man.

"You motherfucker," said Andre. "So now I've found you."

Andre checked that his silver AK 47 was loaded and working. It was.

"Why did you do this? Why attack my people?"

Kirill was standing in front of a kitchen, no more than thirty metres away. He appeared to be unarmed, but Andre would not take any chances.

Kirill said, "You shot at me first. You injured a good friend of mine. I probably could have let that go, but when I found out you were killing the other survivors in the city, I had to do something. I cannot allow you to kill Russian citizens." Here, Kirill smiled warmly. "After all, I'm just a concerned citizen, doing his best for society."

"We've met before, Kirill, although I can see in your face that you don't recognise me. It's incredible that now you have brought this upon my people."

"The world is an amazing place," said Kirill.

Andre's face remained calm. He moved the gun up quickly, firing the machine gun, but it only tore up the wall behind Kirill who ducked and fled through the kitchen door, bullets smashing into the concrete around him, narrowly avoiding murdering him. The kitchen door swung closed.

Andre held the gun trained at the door.

"Did I hit you, you bastard? I can't see how you would have escaped that."

Andre quickly reached into his pocket and took out a fresh clip for the AK 47. He ejected the old magazine and put that in his pocket on the other side. He checked to make sure the gun was working.

"Good to rock 'n' roll," he said.

He paused for a moment. He could call for his guys to come and provide support while he pursued the Nightmare Man, but his people were busy defending the walls, keeping the zombie menace out as best they could. If he pulled anyone away, it would only weaken their defences. Fuck it, he would do this alone. He needed every able-bodied person defending this place, not helping him to kick a door down and kill an unarmed man.

He advanced upon the kitchen door. When he was just outside it, he said, "May God protect you, Masha."

The door flew inwards with one kick. There was the kitchen, stainless steel surfaces, white plates, boxes of food, tiled walls. In that moment, Andre registered three things: first of all that the oven knobs were all turned to full; secondly, that there was a newspaper stuffed into a toaster, and thirdly, he recalled his man's warning about the Nightmare Man just several minutes ago: "We found a trap that must have been set by him."

The newspaper in the toaster combusted and then instantly ignited the gas in the air. The resulting explosion roared towards him, hurling butchers knives that had been left out in the open before it, which cut Andre into twenty separate pieces and then the explosion killed him a split second later.

There was almost nothing recognisable of the New Mafia leader.

Kirill walked slowly towards him. He studied Andre's gun, but it was unuseable as a weapon – the explosion had destroyed the barrel.

He walked calmly out the kitchen. "Have a nice day, motherfucker," said the Nightmare Man.

He eyed the staircase that would take him to the first floor. "Alright, Karl, you're next."

41.

Anton watched from the relative safety of the bar. Everything inside him screamed for him to run and hide, but he was trying to embrace the fear now. He held up the Nightmare Man's blade. He couldn't help but think that it had some protective quality about it, like some kind of blessed artifact that would work to protect him. It had been used for slicing God knew how many of the Nightmare Man's enemies before, but now hopefully, it would help him cut down a few zombies.

He watched as Kirill ran as fast as he could, closing the gap between him and Karl. There was too much noise from guns and explosions for Karl to even be aware of the incredible danger he was in. Anton realised he was holding his breath. He relaxed. Looking inwards, he discovered that he hoped Karl was killed by the Nightmare Man.

Someone moved behind him and Anton turned, utterly terrified, but standing his ground. He held the knife before him. It shook wildly in his hand. His whole body was shaking.

A person in burned, fuming clothing was there.

"Oh, shit, you're alive …" said Anton.

"Cut the fucking bullshit, you crazy son of a bitch," said the smoldering figure. "And pour me a fucking drink."

Anton's hands shook as he poured a glass of whiskey. He spilled half of it. He used both hands to hand the glass over to keep from dropping it.

It was gone in one gulp. The glass was slammed down on the counter. Anton's uncle stood straighter, invigorated. He had blisters over some of his face and a bleeding cut across his forehead and his clothes were covered in dust from debris and were burned, but he was still very much alive.

"It seems you can't keep a good *medved* down," said The Bear. He held up a rocket launcher, the type of thing that looked like it was designed to destroy an aircraft from the ground. He checked to make sure it was functional.

"And now I am going to kill the Nightmare Man."

42.

THEN

Boris was a businessman. He dealt with the oil contracts in Siberia, helping with pipelines and exploratory projects. Although not an athletic man, he was mentally driven, always willing to put in the extra hours and weekends away from his wife and child if it meant serving the company. That's how he had worked his way up. Just two short years ago, he had been an unemployed alcoholic, drinking until he threw up over himself, often too drunk to even stagger to the toilet. Then he had met Lena and it had changed him. She was a beautiful and determined young woman, working in a high-paying job. She went with Boris because of the demographic that said there were three women to every one man in the region; if Lena didn't have Boris, she wouldn't have any man. To her, it was better to be with an unemployed alcoholic than to have no man at all.

Having such a beautiful girlfriend sparked something inside Boris. He said a prayer to God in gratitude for blessing him with his partner and then he set to work improving himself. It began with him hiring a nice suit and tie to go to interviews. He used his small laptop to study at home every night, at first getting a job in a small office where his newfound enthusiasm meant that he rapidly worked his way up. He constantly taught himself new skills and took an active interest in what the company and managers were doing. Before he knew it, he was a representative for an oil company. He couldn't believe it, but he also knew it had nothing to do with luck – Boris had worked hard to get to where he was.

He was staying in a hotel one evening, nothing fancy, but it was still more money than an average person's monthly wages to stay there for one night. There was a knock on the door. Boris folded the laptop closed, protective of his work. He studied the door for several moments as though he would soon gain the ability to see through doors. He pushed away from the desk and walked across the floor in his socked feet. There were his casual clothes and a pizza box dropped on the floor – his old habits of being a slob at home had not disappeared entirely.

Boris reached the door and looked through the spy hole. An attractive young woman was on the other side. Curious, he unbolted the door and swung it wide open. Suddenly, three large men appeared beside the young woman. They wore hostile glares. In a moment, they were in Boris's hotel room.

Boris backed up, regarding each man calmly. The young woman gently closed the door behind them.

The men were well dressed. Their faces were lean and hard. No mercy there. One of the men, Baldie, spoke, "We already know who you are. We represent the local Mafia. Anyone who does business in the region needs to deal with us. And you, my friend, are making quite a lot of money."

"Actually, my wage is quite modest compared to what the company makes –"

"I do not give a shit. The point is you are making serious money for your organisation. That's where we come in. If you would like things to continue to run smoothly, then you will deal with us. We take a cut of your pay and no one gets hurt."

Boris held his hands up. "Wait a minute, we've done nothing to you. We're just here to do some business, that's all."

"This is not a negotiation," Baldie said. "We have the upper hand here. We can hurt your organisation in all kinds of ways. You have workers that travel here and need to make it to work safely. You have supply trucks you need to be able to rely on. You yourself were not difficult to find."

"Doesn't sound like much of a deal to me," said Boris.

Baldie pulled back his suit jacket. There was a gun on his hip. The other two men were similarly armed.

"We will visit you again in three days," said Baldie. "You better be willing to co-operate. We take ten percent of what you make here or your wife and kids will never see you again."

They left. Boris sat down on the bed. He was shaken but still able to think clearly.

He looked to the hotel fridge. There was alcohol inside. He looked away. No. This was not the time for returning to old habits. A clear head was absolutely essential now. Thoughts were rushing through his mind. Who could he contact? The police? If these men were who they said they were, and Boris had no doubt they were genuine, then going to the police would be a real mistake. After thinking it over for two hours, he knew there was only one man he could call. The only person who would be able to make the Mafia back off.

Boris picked up his phone and called the Nightmare Man.

"Hello, Boris," said Kirill. "How are you, my friend?"

"Not good at all. Kirill, I really need your help. I'm in a hotel in Chelyabinsk. I just had a visit from three men saying they were from the Mafia. They're trying to steal money from us."

"Mafia, you say. Hmmm. Sounds like their strategy."

"Is there anything you can do?"

"I can introduce you to some bodyguards. These guys are from my line of work. They will keep you safe," said Kirill.

"The Mafia guys are not just threatening me; they said they would go after the workers as well. You know, guys just trying to make some money on the new pipeline."

"Well, in that case, I need to arrange a meeting with the Mafia. See if we can't work this out."

"Thanks, Kirill. I don't know what the hell I would do without you."

"Speak to you soon, my friend."

Kirill hung up. Boris sat in the hotel room. He ordered room service but just picked at the food.

The next day, the Mafia received a very special visitor.

In an expensive apartment overlooking the river, six Mafia men sat at a table. They had an unopened bottle of imported champagne and a silver tray of *ikra* and fresh fruit before them. They controlled the crime in the region. The most senior man, Artom, spoke to the others.

"My brothers, we are here to discuss business with someone serious. It seems we've upset him without meaning to."

"Yeah? Who is he?" one of the other men asked, helping himself to some caviar.

Artom said, "The Captain of the Spetsnaz."

The double wooden doors opened and Kirill was led inside. He was dressed in simple athletic attire, almost as though he was on the way to the gym.

"Gentlemen, it's nice to see you. My name is Kirill. I am hoping we can talk things over."

All six of the Mafia men got up from their chairs. Artom gestured to an empty seat. There were three empty seats in total. Artom had expected Kirill to bring company.

Kirill took his chair calmly and sat with his hands folded on the table.

"It is a pleasure to have you here," said Artom. "What exactly can we help you with?"

"It's my friend, a businessman named Boris. He's not a criminal, just a regular guy. He's involved in the pipeline that's being put together here. Last night, three of your people visited him in his hotel room."

"Ah, I see now. My friend, I mean no disrespect, but that is how things are done here. Anyone who wants to run a successful business here needs to be involved with us, to some degree. It's nothing personal. Just the cost of business."

Suddenly, Kirill stood up. "This guy is different. You stay away from him, you hear? If you go anywhere near him, then you will get another visit from me, but next time, I will bring my associates. Is that understood?"

"Yes, you've made yourself perfectly clear."

"I'll find my own way out."

When Kirill was gone, Artom sat with his guys. One of them said, "Can we just kill him?" "Kill the Captain of the Special Forces?" said Artom. "Do you know they call him the Nightmare Man? Even if we could kill him, and that guy is no pussy cat; we would have every Spetsnaz guy in Russia coming to kill us. Killing the Nightmare Man would be literally the last thing we ever did."

"So we go along with this, then. We let that piece of shit push us around."

Artom raised his eyebrows. "That's not what I'm saying. But we can't just blunder in with this guy. If we handle this in the wrong way, then we all die."

"I don't know, boss," said another man. "Maybe we should just leave this one alone. He's a dangerous man. We won't lose any credibility for backing down on this one."

Artom considered. He could indeed let Kirill go and instruct his people to stay away from Kirill's businessman friend. Truth be told, no one was likely to ever find out.

Artom reached for the bottle of champagne.

"My brothers, I have the solution. The Nightmare Man will not go unpunished. He will suffer for disrespecting us in our own house. Best of all, he won't be certain who is hurting him or why."

Three weeks later, Kirill was in a nightclub in Chelyabinsk. The music was typical Western rock and popular music. The beer was mostly German. The food was a mixture of Chinese and Italian. A number of people sat at tables smoking sheesha, a type of large bottle with water in it that filtered the tobacco smoke for anyone who breathed from the tubes extending out of the device.

Kirill moved through the crowd. He wore smart casual clothes that were loose and would allow him to move freely if he had to fight.

On several podiums, beautiful girls danced slowly, their movements accentuated their curves. The girls looked amazing, but that was common for girls in Russia. Kirill watched them for a moment and then moved on.

At the bar, a man sat with about six empty beer and spirit glasses around him. Kirill rested a hand on the man's back and he lifted his head slowly to face Kirill. The man was obviously intoxicated, but he was also athletic and looked capable.

"Hi, Kirill," the man said. "Haven't seen you in a while. You keeping busy? Join me for a drink. Waitress, two more of these, thanks."

"No thanks, I don't drink."

"Come on, you can join your own brother for a drink. We got to catch up. I hardly ever see you anymore."

"Fine," said Kirill. "A glass of coke, then."

His brother laughed. "Come on! Have a real drink. Something that's bad for you."

"That is bad for me."

His brother sighed and signaled to the waitress to just bring one drink instead.

"So what have you been doing anyway?"

Kirill leaned on the bar. "I had some business to take care of after Volgograd. Me and my work colleagues had to visit some bad people. But that's all been taken care of now."

"Glad to hear it." His brother raised a glass to him.

"And how have you been keeping? Not drinking like this all the time, I hope?"

"No, I train most days. It's just when I have one drink I find it hard to stop. Are you sure you won't join me for one?"

Kirill shook his head. "When do you go back to work?"

His brother thought for a moment, which in his drunken state looked like an effort. "Next week. I'm just trying to make the most of my time off before I go back to catching bad guys."

Suddenly, someone bumped into Kirill. He turned like lightning, ready to destroy the threat. An apologetic young man held his hands up. "Hey, I'm sorry, man! I'm really sorry. I tripped. I just had too much to drink. I'm so sorry."

Kirill held his hands up ready to strike the young man and anyone else who was a threat but it appeared to be a genuinely innocent situation. He allowed the young man to walk away.

The young man walked out the nightclub. His job was done. His name was Andre, at this time just a middle-level Mafia man. He walked up to two police officers.

"Hey, *politsia*! Help!"

The two middle-aged men looked concerned. "What is it?" asked one.

Andre said, "There's a man in there selling drugs. I saw him dealing to someone in the toilets. When they saw me, they threatened to kill me. So I ran out here. I'm glad I found you guys."

The two policeman looked through the glass doors into the nightclub.

"Which man is it?"

Andre said, "Well-built guy at the bar. Looks like he means business. You can't miss him."

"Alright, we'll check it out," said one policeman. "But you're not going anywhere. You stay right here, understood?"

"Hey, I swear I'm not going anywhere," said Andre.

Inside the nightclub, Kirill's coke had arrived. He thanked the waitress.

"So," Kirill had a sip of his drink, "are we going out for dinner tomorrow night? I'd really like to meet this young woman you've been seeing."

Suddenly, two policeman were behind Kirill. He turned calmly, still holding his glass.

"Good evening, officers, how can I help you?"

"I'm sorry to disturb you, sir, but I need to ask you to empty your pockets."

"Why? What's going on?"

"Sir, empty your pockets, please. I just need to see what you are carrying, then you can enjoy the rest of your night."

Kirill's brother said, "Hey, guys, I know this man. He is definitely not a criminal. Now I suggest you leave him alone. He's someone you really don't want to get involved with."

"Sir, your pockets. I need to see what's in them."

Kirill turned to his brother. "Relax, I haven't done anything wrong. I'm sure they've got me confused with someone else."

Kirill reached into his pocket, feeling a strange packet there. He took it out. It was a taped bag full of powder.

In prison, Kirill always maintained that he was innocent, that someone must have planted the heroin on him. He could not be sure, but he had his suspicions of who was involved. He was stripped of his title of a Captain of Spetsnaz and sentenced to ten years in prison in Siberia. Only recently before he was found with drugs, Kirill had led a mission of vengeance against the perpetrators of the Volgograd bombing. This was a classified mission, as so much of his work was, but the end result was that he and his men slaughtered everyone even remotely involved in the terrorist attack which killed Russian citizens. For this, Kirill received praise from the Russian President himself in private, shaking hands with him. He had also been saluted by the Spetsnaz.

43.

NOW

Karl walked with his bodyguard on the first floor, approaching the foyer. The sounds of battle were all around. Karl was smiling.

Karl's bodyguard fell unconscious and Karl turned to see the Nightmare Man beside him. One punch and Karl's nose was broken. His hands went to his face but Kirill was quicker, snatching Karl in a headlock, ready to snap his neck.

Karl struggled to breathe. "Wait a minute, we can talk about this."

"Nothing to talk about. I'm going to break your neck and feed you to the zombies. You won't be able to escape, just watch while they eat you alive."

Kirill walked him closer to the balcony, ready to throw him off. As he was about to end Karl's life, he felt a pain in his arm. He flinched, loosening his grip on Karl. Looking back, he saw a woman there, a dentist, holding a scalpel. Karl managed to slide free, saying, "Meet my new apprentice!"

Kirill growled and punched The Dentist in the face. Her head snapped back violently and she was out cold. Kirill looked to the KGB officer who had wisely chosen to run away, going for the pistol on his belt. He fired, missing. Kirill was moving, rolling across the floor. Two more bullets missed. He calculated the distance between him and Karl. He couldn't make it before being shot. Kirill leapt off the balcony, down to the floor below. He looked up as Karl ran to the edge, blood streaming down his face, firing again but this time out of bullets.

Kirill growled. Nothing he could do right now. He was close to where the six Mafia bosses were penned in, in the foyer. They strained at their cage, trying to reach Kirill.

Kirill was aware of someone else nearby. He turned to see The Bear holding a rocket launcher up to his shoulder.

The Bear said, "Alright, you bastard, take this."

The rocket flew from the barrel, pouring smoke as it gathered speed. Kirill's reflexes were good. He dropped to the floor and the rocket sailed harmlessly overhead. However, it then connected with the zombie enclosure and exploded, the blast stunning Kirill.

Dazed, he got to his feet again, only to find he was now surrounded by the six Mafia boss zombies. The first one charged in, determined to bite his neck, but Karl chose that moment to fire at the Nightmare Man and the bullet that was meant to kill him instead struck the zombie in the back of its head, dropping it instantly.

Another zombie, Artom, seized Kirill's wrist. Artom brought his teeth down, but a split second before he could bite Kirill, he was punched in the face, his jaw flying away like a rotting horse shoe. He stood up as if confused. Another zombie seized Kirill's wrist, three bullets smashed into its back from where Karl fired one level up. The zombie was momentarily shaken, allowing Kirill to break free. He would have made it away, but another zombie blocked his path. Normally, this would have been no problem for him, but he was still stunned by the rocket explosion, and so it was with a dream-like quality he watched as the zombie bit his wrist.

The pain was fire.

He screamed in rage, punching the zombie's head clean off its shoulders. The headless body stood there for a moment before falling. Then another zombie was on him, this time biting his other forearm. He flung the zombie through the air and it landed some distance away, breaking its spine.

Kirill looked at his two bleeding arms. Maybe he could –

Another zombie bit him, this time in the neck. Kirill cried out and flung his body violently forward, almost as if sneezing. The zombie was thrown overhead and landed on the floor. Kirill held his neck. Crimson blood spilt between his fingers.

Mafia guys had arrived and they seemed to know he was the man who had caused all this, the deaths of their friends. They began shooting, so he ran, pulling obstacles behind him and trying to block the way.

Eventually, he was safe, or at least safe enough to survey the damage. Both his arms were bitten. There was the possibility of amputating the infected parts, of still surviving this, but worst of all was the bite in his neck, which couldn't obviously be amputated without killing himself.

He snarled in rage and frustration. He was dead. The only thing left to do was to make his enemies pay as dearly as possible.

"I'll kill every fucking one of you myself."

He raged, breaking up a bathroom cupboard and taking some dressings out. As he held a bandage to his neck, he noticed something else. A container of liquid nitrogen. An idea came into his head to stop the bleeding, and maybe even stop the spread of the zombie infection.

Kirill opened the container and splashed liquid nitrogen on the bites on his wrists. The bleeding stopped. The bites were frozen. Cords stood out in his wrists. It hurt.

Next, he splashed the liquid nitrogen on his neck. Again, the wound froze. The bleeding had stopped. He had no idea if that would stop the infection – after all, it had already gotten into his bloodstream –but at least he wouldn't bleed out.

Kirill found the detonator in his pocket. He still had options. He noticed a statue of Jesus on the cross. It had not been desecrated at all by the Mafia guys during their stay here. Looking at it, Kirill remembered Sasha's speech about forgiving your enemies. Above the statue was a video camera. It seemed to be focused right on him.

Someone was coming. Kirill got to his feet – this simple act was an enormous effort now. He hid behind a doorway and then saw who it was. Semyon.

"Hey," Kirill said weakly.

Semyon froze, halfway in the motion of fleeing, before he realised it was Kirill.

"Oh my God – Kirill …oh, no …you've been bitten."

"I haven't got long left, Semyon. All that's left to do is sell my life as dearly as possible. Now, I have a job for you."

44.

THEN …

The weights flew into the air. He held them up, gathering his spirit, and slowly lowered the barbell to his chest. It had barely touched him when he shoved the weight away from him again.

Nearby, Harley was talking to Ross. It was difficult to hear them over the sounds of the boxing gym, heavy bags being hit and swinging, creaking on chains, people skipping rope, people in the ring sparring.

Ross said, "The guy owes me money. I want him beaten for it, something he will always remember."

Harley was overweight, but in his younger days had been an athletic boxer. Years of high-intensity training and high-caloric eating had turned to mush almost overnight when he had retired as a fighter and become a coach instead, ordering the young lads around and directing them in their training. Still, his appearance was deceiving – he could still knock any man out with one punch.

"Hey, no problem. I'll put a couple of lads here on it. They go to his house late at night, bust the door in, and then bust his head in. He'll see sense after that. And realise that he stole money from the wrong person."

Ross considered it. "I don't know. This man is a tough guy, used to working security. He likely sees taking a beating as just another occupational hazard."

Ivan put the weights back on the rack. He sat up. Hands on his knees. He was breathing heavily. "Let me do it. I'll sort him out."

Ross could barely hear Ivan over the slap of leather punching gloves hitting heavy bags. "He needs something psychological, something that will really fuck with him."

Ivan had a rat-like face, sleek; his body had no fat and instead was all chiselled muscle. "Simple. I'll go over there and rape him."

Ross looked back to Harley, who was taking Ivan's proposal seriously "You would do that?"

"Sure," said Ivan. "The job calls for him to get the message. He won't forget me. I promise."

In the boxing ring, two fighters slowly circled each other, hands up protecting their heads. They each threw out left jabs, testing the other's defenses, searching for vulnerabilities. One fighter made a mistake, his guard coming low, and this was immediately exploited by the other man who landed a punch on his face.

Ivan was on his feet now. His singlet top clung to his sweaty body.

"So what's it going to be? Do we have a deal?"

Ross looked to Harley and Ivan, "I want you two to work together on this. Clear?"

"You got it, boss," said Harley. "We're the right men for the job."

Ross laughed and patted both men on the shoulder. "Great! I knew I could rely on you both. I'll leave the details in your hands. Just let me know when it's all over with."

Ross turned and walked out of the boxing gym.

Three months later, Ivan and Harley were in the boxing gym at night. Ivan was working the speed bag, his bandaged hands striking the bag which struck its wooden base and rebounded with blinding speed, but he always seemed to strike it again with perfect timing. He seemed almost bored as he punched his target.

Harley was carrying some old gear, a mixture of old boxing gloves and skipping ropes.

"Hey, Ivan, remember that guy we raped?"

Ivan struck the speed bag with a heavy punch, leaving the bag rebounding for several moments.

"Yeah, the tough guy," he said, turning to face Harley. "I hoped he learned it's wrong to steal from people. How's he doing? Still robbing people?"

"Don't think so. He's dead."

Ivan looked surprised. "Yeah? What happened?"

"He killed himself."

"Holy shit!" Ivan sat down on a bench, head down. He looked first right, then left.

"Wow!" he said. "I wasn't expecting that."

"That's what you get," said Harley. "He shouldn't have done what he did."

"No, he shouldn't have."

Outside, there was a scream. The sounds of people running through the streets.

"What the fuck was that?" asked Harley.

They both went to the window. Outside in the dark street, people were running from a thin crowd of strange people with bite marks and wounds on them. The zombies moved slowly, their quest for their next meal never ending.

"What the hell is going on out there?" Ivan asked.

"Shit, I just saw some person on fire."

"It's chaos everywhere, people chasing and killing each other." Ivan held the bars on the window to lever himself up for a better view. A searchlight shone briefly through the window, bathing his face in cold light. There were sirens and the sounds of gunfire. By now, other boxers had stopped training to see what was going on outside. There was general muttering concern and confusion. Some people tried their mobile phones only to find they did not work.

Harley said, "It looks like the end of civilisation as we know it."

Very slowly, Harley and Ivan looked towards each other. Then they both laughed and high-fived each other.

Twelve weeks later, Ivan and Harley were in the city of Chelyabinsk, a wall around the city now. Snow was falling. The streets were cold. Armies of zombies prowled the roads and were an ever-present danger. They lurked in every building. Harley and Ivan were right at home in this new environment. In many ways, this cold dangerous landscape reflected their own minds, their own dark souls cast into hellish un-life. They had never been happier.

Ivan kicked the door of an apartment open. He was carrying a bag of groceries. "Honey, I'm home!"

Harley laughed. He walked in behind Ivan carrying a broadsword casually over his shoulder. It was streaked with blood.

Ivan set the groceries down on the counter where they overbalanced and spilt on the floor, some cans of soup rolling noisily and long packets of pasta sliding out. Ivan kicked a bag of dumplings out the way. It slid across the kitchen floor and came to a stop when it collided with a cat's bowl, bone dry now.

"Been a quiet day, Harley. We haven't even seen anybody in two days now."

"They're still out there. The people who are good at hiding will be the last ones to go. I'm sure there're loads of people left. There may even be communities doing quite well."

"Are you fucking playing with me?" Ivan said through munching an apple. "Only a psychopath could survive out there."

"Which is why we're doing so well!"

Ivan laughed and sprayed pieces of apple like foam. "Yeah, that's true."

Ivan went into the bedroom. There was a woman with her hands bound above her head, secured by a length of chain connected to the ceiling. She was wearing an oversized shirt belonging to a man, barely concealing her. Tangled hair fell over terrified eyes. She was probably in her late thirties, still attractive. A silk tie had been used to gag her, but she still cried out when she saw Ivan, trying to retreat although her binds made it impossible.

"Did you think I forgot you, sweetheart?" Ivan held her jaw in one calloused hand. "Nah, wouldn't happen. I've had you on my mind all day."

The young woman cried out again. Harley came into the room, regarding her with interest. Then he said, "You shouldn't open your door to strangers, *deyushka*. Not even during a zombie apocalypse."

"Hell, *especially* during a zombie apocalypse!" said Ivan. Both men laughed.

Later, Harley and Ivan were talking to Andre, the leader of the New Mafia. They were in the foyer of the Tank Academy, surrounded by Mafia killers. In the centre of the room was a homemade cage containing six zombies. Ivan regarded the caged monsters and then turned to Andre.

"You sure have an eye for decorating. Not sure I'd like to feed your pets, though."

"Then don't piss me off," said Andre. Ivan's eyes flared for a moment, the rage of a killer who is used to inflicting his will on others, but then calmed down. His jaw muscles relaxed. This was not a fight he could win.

Andre said, "I have work for you, sure. Be very clear you understand that I am in charge here. If you ever try to cross me, I can have you shot from ten blocks away. Only it won't be a head shot." Andre smiled towards the six caged zombies.

"Hey, we are totally on board," said Harley. "When you work with us, you get two of the best. We won't let you down, Andre."

The New Mafia boss nodded. "I'll watch with great interest then while you carry out your first assignment."

The two men walked away. As they passed the enclosure with the Mafia zombies inside, Ivan stopped. Artom, who had been a Mafia boss in life, was straining through the metal to reach him.

Ivan regarded him for long moments.

"You tried to help me when no one else would. Anyone else would have left me in prison. But you always had my back, you gave me my freedom again. I'm sorry to see you like this, comrade."

He left.

Their first mission was a surveillance role. They were holed up in an apartment overlooking the river. Harley had the binoculars pressed to his eyes with one hand; he was munching an energy bar and tearing it away with his other hand as his teeth clamped into it. The room was dark, dirty.

"Yeah, that's it, you son of a bitch," Harley said, "I see you."

"What do you see?" Ivan dragged savagely on a cigarette. His tank top showed off his flawless abs.

"A young malchik, running through the streets. It's the same guy every day, gathering supplies and then running off. Yeah, there he goes."

"You can keep an eye out there and watch everything that's going on. I'm going to stay focused right here." He cast his eyes downwards at the two young people bound on the floor, a boy and girl, mid-twenties; they had been foolish enough to let two strangers in "distress" into their home. Now they regretted their decision, tears flooded down their faces. Both knew what Ivan and Harley had in store for them.

"You know, I could have been a champion fighter." Ivan held up a carving knife. It gleamed as he appraised it, momentarily lighting his eyes.

"I was really good. Got up every day at six am to do my roadwork. Ran 10k every day. I could do twenty pull-ups. I turned up to every class, sometimes training four times a day. Would have been a champion, you know, if I hadn't gone to prison."

He held up his right fist. The knuckles were tight and hard.

"Know what they call this?"

The young couple cried unintelligibly through their gags. Eyes wide.

"The hammer. That's what they called it. Because if I hit you with a right cross, it was like I had taken a hammer to your face. And make no mistake, I did that to a lot of people. Both in and out of the ring. See, I was a man for hire. I gave results. If you had the right money and you wanted someone hurt, I could make it happen. I was good at that, too."

He held the carving knife up with his left hand. "But I'm even better at cutting people. That's something I have a gift for. I was a butcher's apprentice, see. It helped pay the bills and allow me to keep boxing. I sure carved up a lot of animals. Funny thing is, if you stand a sheep up on its hind legs, it's basically the same as a person. Real easy to cut through."

Ivan held the blade before the boy's eyes. "You get to watch while I do your girl. Trust me, you're going to like this, you'll see how a real man does a girl."

To the young woman, he said, "You like me, don't you? Shit, I like you. I like you a real lot. Anyone can fucking see that. There's so much I want you to feel. I'm going to teach you a lesson, girl, in the worst possible way."

He loomed forward with the knife, teeth bared, seizing the girl's dark hair painfully so that it was almost yanked out of her scalp. Her eyes bulged and neck veins stood up. She wet herself. Fluid pooled around her.

"Shit! We got him!" said Harley.

"What are you on about?"

"The fucking tough guy, he's talking to that kid who goes gathering supplies all the time. Seems the two of them are friends."

A look of disappointed confusion was on Ivan's face.

"Grab your kit and let's go." Harley picked up his jacket as he walked away from the window, for it was cold in Chelyabinsk. "The Nightmare Man's riding out on a motorcycle. We better not let him out of our sight."

Ivan sighed deeply. "Some fucking bastard is stopping my fun. Okay. Your lucky day."

He stood in a lightning movement, agile as a cat, regarding the hostages thoughtfully, then flung the knife into the floor. It landed in the floorboards and thrummed for a few moments between them.

"Take care of yourselves, kids, and don't go fucking letting people you don't know into your home," Ivan said as he left. He closed the door behind him.

Days later, they were back at the Tank Academy, downing beers. Ivan had his feet up on the table. Harley was too heavy to do that so he sat with his hands on his knees, the binoculars slung around his neck.

"I can't believe we lost that fucking bastard," said Ivan to his beer. "Then again, he had a motorcycle."

"You know, it's the weirdest thing," said Harley, "I saw these zombies with vests on."

"Well, they all dress differently. People are people. I saw two zombies in bondage gear the other day. Hah!"

"Nah, man, it was like they had bombs in the vests or something."

Ivan put his feet down. "You mean like homicide bombers or something?"

Harley nodded thoughtfully. "Yeah, like that."

"How many were there?"

Harley considered this. "A few. Maybe more. I see a lot through these binoculars."

"Where'd you see them?"

"Near the river, mostly. Some were just outside here. You think I ought to say something to Andre?"

Ivan put his beer down. He took out a stick of gum, removed it from its foil packet, leaned back in his chair so it was on two legs, put his feet on the table, and fed the stick of gum onto his tongue. He chewed a few times and then smiled.

"No, why worry the man unnecessarily?"

45.

NOW …

In the foyer, there was a tense standoff between The Bear's men and the Mafia. The hunters and prison guards were dressed in simple clothing, often with at least some animal pelts on them. The Mafia were all about style, wearing sharp suits and extravagant jewelry. The Bear's men huddled together, terrified of the Mafia who all had to be professional killers to have made it this far.

Karl called out, "We don't need to fight. The man who caused all this is nearby. I know you've lost some people. So have we. And it is all one man's fault. Kirill."

Karl turned to The Bear, who stood with the spent rocket launcher at his side. "I told you I would kill him. Now, it is as good as done. Kirill does not have long left to live."

The Bear dropped the rocket launcher on the floor. It made a hollow metallic clang.

"You did well. Really fucking well."

The Mafia guys studied the exchange between the KGB agent and the prison warden. More zombies were closing in.

"Freeze, motherfuckers."

It was the Nightmare Man. He stopped in a doorway, blood drenching his clothes; he was battered but not defeated.

Karl grinned wildly. The Bear registered surprise. Masha coolly turned her rifle to face Kirill.

The Bear said, "Who the fuck are you, Kirill? We chased you across fucking Siberia and through a city of the living dead and you're still alive."

"He's almost dead now," said Karl, still grinning. "The clock is ticking extremely fast. What have you got to say, Kirill?"

Masha lifted her head away from the riflescope. "I'm going to shoot all your important pieces off, then I'll leave you for the zombies to finish. My family will rest a little easier knowing the end was painful and terrifying for you."

Kirill was breathing raggedly. The large foyer had gone almost silent. The New Mafia and The Bear's men waited, The Bear, Karl, and Masha ready to kill the Nightmare Man the moment he tried anything.

The Nightmare Man held up a detonator.

"If I let go of this, you're all dead," he said. "If you shoot me, you die."

Masha was about to laugh but then she looked around – they were surrounded by zombies, a large number of them wearing explosive vests. The Bear woke up to the danger. "Fuck. We're surrounded."

Karl's eyes were wide above his bleeding nose. All his arrogance had vanished.

A young man joined Kirill, saying, "It's all done. I've put explosives on the floor above. If the bombs go off, everyone in this room dies."

"You did a good job, Semyon. I'm proud of you."

"Would you like to fucking negotiate?" asked The Bear. He seemed curious rather than afraid. "Or are you just going to kill us?"

Kirill looked around the room as if seeing it and all the people in it for the first time. He was pale. Breathing rapidly.

"I'm sorry for the people I killed. Mistakes were made."

Masha brought her gun up in fury but did not fire. Her finger was curled around the trigger.

Kirill continued, "All this … someone else is behind this. The wall around the city. The Spetsnaz outside the wall …those men served under me."

The Bear's eyes widened.

Kirill said, "We've all wronged each other in some way. Now we're in a situation where if we don't work together, then we all die."

"You can't be forgiven," said Masha. "It was my family you killed."

"I'm dead anyway," said the Nightmare Man. "What does it matter if you work with me for a while? Together, we can find out why this happened."

Karl said, "You have got the upper hand here, but the moment we step out of this room, you lose control. We can kill you and not be afraid of your bombs."

"True. But if you don't make a deal with me, then you die right here, right now."

The Bear said, "Sounds like a bargain to me! Let's call a truce."

Karl slowly smiled, "Okay, I'm in. I want to get out of this room alive."

"I still want you dead." Masha had not lowered her rifle.

The Nightmare Man raised the detonator. "Only after we find out what is really happening here. Not before. Medved, take her gun off her."

Masha looked up to see The Bear suddenly beside her; he moved surprisingly fast for a man of such size. The barrel of her gun was seized in one giant paw, and she could not pull away. The Bear took the gun as though he was removing it from a child, saying, "Sorry, but if I don't take your weapon, then we don't even live for one more minute."

The Bear threw the gun over to Kirill. It landed at his feet.

Kirill smiled tiredly as if seeing an old friend. He moved slowly and picked up Masha's rifle. Even with all his injuries he still handled the gun with astonishing grace. Holding the rifle, he looked terrifying, a demon released into a city of lambs.

"Okay," said Kirill, his commanding voice freezing the entire room. "This building is compromised. Every zombie in Chelyabinsk is on its way here. We need to get our people out alive and find a safe destination."

"We still have vehicles," said Masha, "and most of us are fighters."

The Rose Maniac took off her helmet. She was a beautiful young woman. Karl froze; he could not believe what he was seeing so he moved closer.

The troops worked together now, securing weak points, gathering supplies into the vehicles that were left. There was an uneasy sense of unity now, the common knowledge they were all in this together and had to co-operate or else none of them would survive.

Karl could not take his eyes off the Rose Maniac.

She was his sister, Rhyza.

No one saw the tears falling down Karl's face, crying because his sister was one of the Mafia. For long moments, he watched her. Then he wiped the tears away and began to help everyone else evacuate the building.

Anton was still in the bar where the Nightmare Man had left him. He had hidden from a group of zombies that had staggered by, crouching behind the bar, holding the Nightmare Man's knife as though it were a crucifix that could repel vampires. He worked hard to control his breathing. Sweat rolled down his face. He could hear them, the living dead, bumping into things and knocking a painting on the wall down. The crash was lost in the sound of gunfire somewhere else in the building. Finally, the ghouls passed without incident. Anton waited a few more moments then stood up. For a second, he met his own eyes in the mirror behind the bar, frightened but determined.

He looked at the knife in his hand. It was only then he realised how tightly he was gripping the handle. He willed his hand to relax.

His eyes floated to the bar again. The alcohol could be a potential weapon; he could fashion Molotov cocktails out of the bottles if he had to. Further consideration made him reject this, however, because although he could set a few zombies alight the likelihood of the fire spreading and endangering everyone else in the building was high.

Leaning on the bar, he got his breath back. He could not believe how much the adrenalin robbed him of oxygen.

Footsteps. Anton froze, but he registered straight away that these were not the uncoordinated shuffling steps of a zombie, but rather two people running down a corridor. Part of him screamed at himself to hide behind the bar again, to be safe. The more logical part of himself reasoned that since it was two humans approaching, he had nothing to fear.

Two men entered the room. One was overweight, long frizzled hair spilling down his shoulders; he looked like a biker. The other one wore a tank top and was obviously in fantastic physical condition. The two men paused, regarding Anton.

The well-built guy approached Anton. "Greetings, brother." He had his hands wide to show there were no weapons in them. "We come in peace."

Anton was frozen to the spot; he knew something was wrong with these two men but he did not act. Out of politeness.

When he was almost standing next to Anton, the fit man threw out a left jab. Fluid, fast. Like a snake. The stone fist caught Anton in the jaw, rattling his brain, and he fell down. He was barely conscious.

"Nice shot," said the fat man, "I heard that Kirill went this way."

"Sure, we can go after him," the well-built man crouched effortlessly beside Anton, "but do you want to have some fun first?"

The fat guy grinned. "Hell, yeah!"

"Alright!" The well-built man grinned back. It was as if the two men were best friends.

The well-built guy was speaking into Anton's face. "You know, I used to be a boxer before all this happened. That's why you never saw my punch coming. Funny, huh? It was a good life."

Harley checked his machine gun. The mechanism was loud.

Anton carefully looked to where he had dropped the Nightmare Man's knife. It was within reach, but he knew the boxer could move with incredible speed, so he couldn't go for it yet. Maybe when the boxer was distracted somehow he could go for it.

Ivan cradled Anton's jaw in one hand, gentle, almost tender. Anton wanted to believe he wouldn't hurt him. Suddenly, Anton's vision exploded into light. The noise was very loud in his head. Terrifying. He had been punched again.

"Do not go for that knife, comrade," said the boxer. It had caught his attention now so he leaned over to pick it up from the floor. "Hmm, this is really well made. I think I'll keep this."

He looked back to Anton. "You don't mind, do you?"

Anton cringed, expecting to be punched again. "No, it's fine, it's all yours."

Ivan waved the knife at him for a moment. "Thanks."

Harley stood over them both now, machine gun resting on one hip. "I want to punch him till his eyes pop out."

"Well, before we do that, help me get his trousers down."

"No!" cried Anton, trying to get away.

Ivan caught him instantly and punched him in the head again. "If you do what we say, then you will still get out of this alive."

Harley ignored Ivan, unbuckling his belt buckle, "I'm going to fuck you then kill you."

Ivan looked bemused. "Come on, man, I just assured him nothing too bad was going to happen to him, and then you have to go ahead and give the game away."

Anton trembled on the floor.

There were footsteps and someone else came into view. A strongly built woman, she looked as though she would be well suited to ploughing fields. She stopped when she saw the two men looming over Anton.

"Ah, The Dentist," said Ivan. "How about it, deyushka, you want in on this?"

The woman paused before answering, "No, I don't want to help you do what you want to do here."

"Hey, don't be like that," said Harley. "We're just having some fun. You know, you got to do that, or you'll crazy here in the apocalypse."

"Not my cup of tea," said The Dentist.

"So, what are you going to do? You going to try to stop us?"

The Dentist had a gun in her hand. She looked at it as if just realising it was there, "No," she said at last, and began to walk away.

"Please!" Anton called out after her, but she didn't look back. Ivan flung the Nightmare Man's blade so it struck the floor, embedded. He kneeled on Anton, using one knee to drive his face into the floor.

"Shut up, you fucking worm, you'll bring every zombie here –"

The Dentist screamed and all three men looked up sharply to see what was happening. As The Dentist had stepped through the door, a zombie had leapt upon her. It moved fast, not like the vast majority of slow zombies that were easy to outrun. She would have heard it coming if it wasn't for the gunfire nearby.

The zombie was wrapped in barbed wire. Its eyes shone. The Dentist's neck fountained blood as she sank to the floor. A group of the barbed wire zombies filled the doorway, growling, eager to rip the three men to pieces.

Harley steadied his machine gun. "Got it," he said, almost bored. He checked the mechanism on the gun. Ready to rock 'n' roll.

The burst from the gun caught the first zombie in the chest and then Harley corrected, aiming slightly upwards to perforate its skull. The thing shook violently, then its peers cast it forward and trampled over it. The next zombie met a similar fate; its head turned into a target board and the wall behind it was smashed with holes.

Anton was paralysed on the floor. He lay behind Harley, the knife stuck to the floor within arm's reach. The fear was there, again.

It always was.

Ivan was watching the show with interest, seeing his best friend gunning down the zombies. So it came as a complete surprise when Anton's fist smashed into his jaw. There was very little substance to the punch – it was a beginner's punch – but his attention had been focused elsewhere and it was enough to dislodge him from pinning Anton down, leaving him stunned on the floor while Anton scrambled for the knife.

Two more zombies fell to Harley's machine gun. His teeth were bared. Scanning for targets.

The knife plunged into his side.

"What the hell –?"

Harley turned, gazing in astonishment. It was that piece of shit Anton who had stabbed him. That born victim who had just lay there and taken it while Ivan had battered him.

"You?" Harley's eyes were wide. Anton was still on the floor, breathing raggedly. The knife was stuck in Harley's side.

The machine gun came round, pointed at Anton's head.

The zombies reached Harley first. The spray of bullets that should have decapitated Anton instead went inches to the side of his face as the zombies caught up with Harley, biting him, tearing into his body. As he screamed and turned, he fired the machine gun, a blazing hail of bullets ripping up the floor. Ivan came to his senses just in time, kicking away from the bullets and covering his face like a boxer.

Harley was still on his feet, the zombies to the back of him. His large size made it difficult for him to reach behind himself to dislodge the monsters.

Anton got to his feet, running toward Harley and the zombies. For a moment, he locked eyes with one of the zombies that had its fangs buried in Harley's neck. The message in its eyes was very clear – Anton was next.

He grabbed for the machine gun, but even being eaten alive, Harley refused to give it up. That just left the knife in his side. Anton reached for it and took it out. He held the blade up. He had never been in so much as a fist fight before.

The zombies tore Harley around and he saw his death coming. He was taken to the floor by the weight of the zombies pressing down on him.

Ivan was back in charge of himself now.

"You're fucking dead. I'm going to stab you in the neck and leave you out for the zombies to play with."

As he reached out for Anton, he suddenly pulled back – Anton had tried to cut him with the knife.

Ivan laughed. "You are the first person who ever fought back. Usually people are terrified of me."

Anton got to his feet. His nose was bleeding. He was scared. But he was alive.

Ivan was circling him, light on his feet as if this was a boxing match. A zombie leapt on him and he was taken to the floor, pinned. Years of being focused on his boxing opponent in the ring had left Ivan blind to an attack from anywhere else. He was face to face with the snarling muzzle of the monster that wanted to bite his head off. He fought it, but its writhing energy kept him down.

Across the floor, Harley rose the machine gun one last time. It took the top of the head off the zombie. Even as it was destroyed, it still tried to reach Ivan, black blood pouring out of its mouth and splashing into his face. He punched it in the jaw and threw it off him, on his feet in a second.

He saw Harley with three zombies on him. Anton was still there, looking scared out of his mind but still holding the knife.

"Time for Plan B," said Ivan, reaching behind him and taking out a small pistol from the waist of his trousers.

Anton was convinced he would be gunned down where he stood but instead, Ivan pointed the gun at Harley. "Sorry, brother, I'll see you in the afterlife."

He fired once and ended Harley's misery.

When he turned back to Anton, the young man finally began to run. Ivan fired at him five times as he fled to the same door the monsters had come from. The gun clicked dry as Anton escaped.

Ivan looked to the floor again where the zombies were devouring his dead friend. He wiped his face again to get the black blood off it. There was nothing more he could do here.

He fled.

They fought under the leadership of The Bear and the Nightmare Man, both men well experienced in warfare. Now the New Mafia fought alongside The Bear's men, holding the zombies back. Rhyza used her sports car to deliver people safely from the Tank Academy, always speeding back to rescue more people. Masha the sniper provided covering support, picking off any zombie that threatened to get too close to one of the defenders or to one of the escaping vehicles. The twin anti-aircraft guns tore through the zombie crowd, ripping them apart like invisible hands plucking at dough, but it seemed there were always more zombies to surge forward and take their place.

The Nightmare Man and The Bear were two of the last to leave. Kirill said, "Medved, that's almost everyone out of here. Time to go."

"Fuck yourself, Kirill! We wait five minutes more." The Bear was firing a machine gun indiscriminately into the crowd of zombies, ripping apart torsos and limbs. The zombies only stopped moving if they were hit in the brain; otherwise, they kept up their relentless advance.

Kirill was pale, but it seemed that somehow his energy was returning. He held a compact machine gun, teeth bared. The Bear stopped shooting at the monsters but kept watching them, grinning and unaware that Kirill was pointing a gun at his head. They were completely surrounded, zombies smashing in through the windows and overrunning the building. There was an unending sea of hungry corpses, smashing themselves against the building, somehow sensing Kirill and The Bear were inside.

"Uncle."

Both men turned to see Anton there.

"Hey, you made it!" said The Bear.

"Th – thank you for waiting for me."

Anton turned to Kirill. "I … I think this belongs to you."

Anton held out the knife to the Spetsnaz Captain.

Kirill looked from the handle of the blade offered to him back to Anton.

"You're different now," said the Nightmare Man. "You keep it, comrade."

Anton didn't respond. He put the blade through his belt.

"Also," said Kirill, "you're bleeding. We need to give you some medical attention."

Anton looked down at his chest to see five bullet holes in him. His eyes widened, and he fell into the arms of The Bear.

The Medved lay Anton down and tore his shirt up over his chest to expose the wounds, quickly applying wound dressings.

Kirill looked back to The Bear. "If you had been in Spetsnaz, you and me could have done things."

He lifted the gun away so that it rested on his shoulder and then studied the zombies down below.

Downstairs, Rhyza drove her car in, tyres screeching, ghouls flung from before the car and smashing against a distance wall, struggling to stand up again. The car was clogged with blood and gore, some still-moving corpses reaching out weakly from where they had been smashed apart and left on the roof in the pool of carnage; these ghouls were little more than a head and one broken arm. Rhyza opened the driver side door. "They're everywhere now! This is the last time I will be able to drive through them. My wheels are choked with zombies as it is."

"Come on," said Kirill, running towards Rhyza. After a moment, The Bear joined him, carrying Anton in his arms. Kirill opened the passenger door and dove inside. The Bear opened the other door, laying Anton into the back seat of the car, turning back to face the Academy.

"I hope this works," said The Bear.

Before he could get in, a zombie had raced up the back of the car, leaping across the roof and seized his arm. Its grip was strong. Six more fast zombies dropped down from the balcony above, barely slowed from the fall, immediately thrashing to their feet in rage, eyes glowing, and charging The Bear. All seven zombies were wrapped in barbed wire and had railway spikes driven into their limbs and metal clamps over their heads as if they had escaped from electric chairs. Shards of porcelain and jagged nails were exposed in their mouths as they screamed in rage. Whether someone had done this to them or they had inflicted this damage upon themselves was unclear. They were very fast and aggressive.

"Get inside!" screamed Rhyza.

The Bear was pulling at the zombie's grip, but its hands were strong. Then the monster's head exploded. The Bear ducked, released from the iron grip. Within two seconds, the other six zombies lay still, massive holes smashed through their heads. The corpses were spread across the floor, twisted and tangled. The Bear looked over the roof of the car, past the limp monster, to see the Nightmare Man with a smoking gun in his hand. It was aimed at The Bear.

"Damn, and I thought you were dangerous unarmed," said The Bear.

Kirill did not lower the gun. "Get in the fucking car or the next bullet is through your fucking skull."

"You don't need to tell me twice." The Bear was laughing as he climbed into the vehicle.

Rhyza hit the accelerator before The Bear was even fully inside. The car spun over the corpses, spitting up a stream of black blood across the walls. A broken section of wall acted as a ramp as she drove the car over it, sending them airborne. Outside the building, zombies were closing in, drawn to this part of the building by the noise.

Rhyza smashed through the zombies trying to seize them. They burst through the crowd outside, wheels spinning over piles of corpses, mud and snow flying, the car shrieking away. The tyres spun in the snow and corpses, threatening to lose control, but Rhyza was able to command the car, even as it spun and sent monsters flying. Moments later, they were free, the crowd of zombies slowly vanishing in the rearview mirror, the car speeding towards the new dawn.

Once they were away from the horde, the streets were much quieter. The roads were wide, giving them plenty of room to steer around any cars that had been left abandoned. They passed many buildings with the windows smashed in. There were corpses on the footpaths, many of them stripped clean of flesh. Occasionally, there was a stray zombie who heard the car and attempted to give chase but was quickly left behind.

The Bear leaned with his elbows on the two front seats. "So where to next?"

"Megapolis," answered Kirill. "There's a group of survivors staying there. They are not professional fighters, so they could use some protection. And you guys need somewhere to stay. Everyone wins. Simple."

"And you're sure they won't mind having us there?" asked the driver. "I can certainly see how we may have upset a few people recently."

"This is pure survival now. Anything that happened in the past has to be forgiven."

The Bear did not say anything to this, but minutes later, they approached a church and he said, "My sister was married in that church. Ha! I haven't been there in years."

The car slowed as they neared the church, three of the passengers curiously looking out the window, Anton lying unconscious. At first, the church appeared empty, the car park surrounding it cluttered with litter. There were three shops sharing the car park, two of which had smashed windows.

"There's someone there," said Kirill. A man had crept out from behind the church, carrying a pitchfork over his shoulder. Now that he had been seen, he made no attempt to hide. Looking closely, it was apparent there were other people inside the church, although it was impossible to say how many. Three other men emerged from the broken shops, also carrying farming tools. Their stances made it clear that strangers were not welcome.

"That's quite clever," said Kirill. "They leave the outside looking as if this place has been taken over. Meanwhile, people stay inside and keep out of sight. If we hadn't slowed down, we would never have seen that guy with the pitchfork."

"Let's keep moving," said the Rose Maniac, gently pulling the car away. The four men guarding the church watched them leave.

The streets became increasingly residential. At times, it seemed everything was normal, that they were just passing through a quiet street, then suddenly, they would see a burned-out car or a shopfront with the front window broken and a dead body leaning out of it, and they were quickly reminded the nightmare was all too real.

"My home is gone now," said the Rose Maniac. "The *zombi* have taken over. I would give anything to have us all back together again, to be home."

Kirill looked to her. "You can never return to that place."

They drove in silence for a few minutes, then Kirill said, "Medved, I never had anything to do with drugs. The crime they convicted me for, possession of heroin, I am innocent of that crime."

"It doesn't matter now whether you're innocent or not. Like you said, we're all in this together."

They drove on in silence.

Back at the Tank Academy, the zombies still surged forward, the horde desperate to get inside. They still poured through the walls, worming their way through the windows and the jagged holes caused by explosions. They filled the building, looking almost surprised to find no living humans inside. Rotted feet tread on corpses. Some corpses stirred to life to join the ranks of the undead, now brothers with them instead of the New Mafia. The zombies unwittingly smashed expensive bottles of *champonskoe* on the floor, spilling caviar and gold jewelry, fine clothes trampled underfoot, money on the floor now soaked in blood. None of it mattered. They had taken the building; finally, inexorably, they had won.

One zombie seemed to stand out from the rest. In life, he had been a fit and strong man; now, his teeth were bared in rage. The boxer glared at the place where the Nightmare Man had fled in a car minutes before. He ran towards the smashed wall, leaping over the rubble and giving chase. His feet pounded the road, arms pumping furiously as he screamed his fury.

The zombie's triumph was short lived. The Nightmare Man had rigged the building to explode. A loud boom split the sky with a searing flash of light, much like the meteorites that had brought the zombie plague to Chelyabinsk in the first place. The light expanded across the city as the Tank Academy exploded, glass from the handful of intact windows burst outwards. The home of the New Mafia collapsed. Hundreds of tons of concrete were brought down upon the zombies, crushing and destroying them beneath it.

Elsewhere, the last of the New Mafia joined the survivors at the Megapolis. At first, the people were uneasy about allowing the New Mafia to join them, but they saw that Kirill was working with these people; he seemed to trust them, so they would, too.

The Priest said, "In their hour of need, let's open our arms to our brothers. There is room for everybody here. We can all stay in Megapolis."

The survivors in Megapolis shared what little supplies they had with the New Mafia and welcomed them into their home.

Rhyza saw her friend Masha. They were both exhausted from fighting, both covered in blood and gore.

"Masha! We're alive!"

"Yes, we made it."

"I haven't seen Andre. Did he make it? Did you … see what happened?"

"I'm sorry, Rhyza. He did his best for all of us, but he's gone now."

Rhyza's eyes sank. "Who will lead our brothers and sisters now?"

They were both silent for a few moments and then Rhyza said, "We could do it. We can lead the New Mafia from now on."

Masha smiled. "You're right. We'll be in charge of the New Mafia. We'll keep everybody safe."

"You'll make a good leader. You're a kind person."

Both Rhyza and Masha turned to see who had spoken. It was Karl. He had dried blood on his face from where he had been punched by Kirill. Otherwise, he looked as dangerous as ever.

"Hi, Karl, it's a surprise to see you again," said Rhyza. She had been part of the Mafia for a long time now, and the frightened young girl she had once been was long gone. What was left was a soldier determined to protect her people.

"But I've got to say," Rhyza continued, "I'm not as nice as you remember me."

Karl held her gaze for a moment, his expression impossible to read. He lowered his eyes a moment, then immediately his eyes flashed back to hers. "You're right! You're Mafia now. You've got your own family to look after."

He walked away.

Sasha was there. He hobbled out to meet the Nightmare Man, using a crutch made from various pieces of wood taped together. It was the wrong height for him and exaggerated his limp. The bandages on his leg were fresh.

"Kirill! You're alive!" Then Sasha noticed the bites. "Oh, shit, I'm so sorry, man …"

"Never mind that now."

Sasha gathered himself. "Alright. I see you brought the Mafia with you. I bet there's an interesting story behind that. What is it? If you can't beat them, join them? Would you like me to become one of the Mafia, too?"

"I'll explain later. Right now, there's work to be done."

"Okay, okay, man, of course. What's next?"

The Nightmare Man bared his teeth. "We're going to find out who is responsible for all this."

In the distance, smoke poured out of the crater of the Tank Academy, former home of the New Mafia. The Nightmare Man stood with Sasha, The Bear, Anton, and Masha. The New Mafia were unloading trucks and *marshrutkas*, filled with supplies, ready to set up their new home. There was still the occasional zombie who had not been drawn to the Tank Academy, but these were quickly beaten down by the lookouts who were dressed in protective clothing.

"That was a fucking adventure," said The Bear, "but we're alive."

Sasha looked up then, still anxious about the nearby dead. "There's got to be thousands of those zombies left." "Yes, for sure," said Kirill. "They'll be drawn by the noise. But we had time to get away."

"The new place will be a fortress," said The Bear.

Masha glared at the Nightmare Man. "Do you even know what this was about?"

He paused before answering, "I'm not sure what you mean."

Everyone was looking at her now. The Bear said, "This is a victory, *deyushka*. We destroyed a hell of a lot of those biters and we are alive to talk about it."

"The cameras," Masha said.

Still, the group was bewildered.

"Haven't you seen the cameras everywhere?"

"Sure," said Sasha, "but so what? There's no one left to watch them ... is there?"

Masha pointed angrily at a small building with a satellite dish on top of it. They walked towards it, weapons drawn.

The building was just a utility shack, but on the roof there was a signal dish.

"I don't think this means anything," said Anton. "I mean, in the past, it might have done something. But Sasha's right, there's no one left to watch."

"Take another look," Sasha said quietly.

On one of the control panels was written:

Dom 3

"I've been away for a long time," said Kirill. "Does that mean something?"

Sasha said, "There is a TV show called Dom 2. It's about a group of people living in a house and everything they do is on camera. The whole nation watches. It's very popular."

"It could just be a coincidence," said Kirill. "Those words could mean   something   else."
"I thought so, too," said Masha, opening her backpack and taking a laptop out. She plugged it into the control panel with a cable, "but then I tried doing this. I'm good with computers, but there was no hacking involved. It's as if they wanted us to see."

Everyone gathered around the computer. The screen lit up and showed various parts of the city, staying on a view for several seconds before randomly displaying another location. Generally, the streets were empty but some of them showed zombies, moving as if drawn to something. Suddenly, the screen changed and showed the image of the survivors gathered around the computer, as if someone was recording them from nearby.

"Who's filming us?" Sasha asked. The Nightmare Man pointed towards a surveillance camera facing them on a nearby building.

"What's the meaning of this, deyushka?" asked The Bear.

But it was the Nightmare Man who spoke. "We're being watched. This whole thing, everything we went through … it's just entertainment," he looked to Masha, "right?"

She smiled grimly. "Yes, that's how it looks to me."

As realisation sunk in for each person, their faces showed first bewilderment and then despair. All their suffering had been for someone else's entertainment.

The Nightmare Man grinned, but it was not a grin that Sasha liked. The Nightmare Man said, "They want a show, so let's give them a fucking show."

PART 3
ZOMBI

LOST FOOTAGE:

Kirill stumbled through the door, bitten and bleeding. "You motherfuckers," he snarled, teeth bared like a wild animal. He had just been bitten by the Mafia boss zombies moments before and was now fleeing the New Mafia.

He staggered; the imperative was to create distance – there was no such thing as safety anymore. Bursting through a door, he closed it behind him, desperate for some way to barricade it; there was none. He was in a kitchen. The Nightmare Man collapsed.

A Spetsnaz soldier leaned calmly against the wall, watching Kirill with amusement. It was Vladimir, from outside the wall enclosing the city.

"You're still alive, even after all this." There was admiration in Vladimir's voice.

"Vladimir? You've got to help me out. There's got to be a hundred people trying to kill me."

"More than that," said the soldier. There was a camera in the corner of the room. Lightning fast, he turned and shot it, exploding it into fragments of plastic and pulverised electronics. He held the smoking gun for a moment as if the shattered remains of the camera may still be some threat before turning back to Kirill. He did not put the gun away.

Hidden at an angle low to the floor was a less obvious camera which continued to record everything.

"Vladimir, its game over for me."

The soldier looked down, as if mentally arguing something with himself.

"Kirill, I always enjoyed being your sergeant. You and me could have done anything."

Moving like a predatory animal, he swiftly unbuckled his satchel, removing a piece of equipment that looked like a cross between a gun and a syringe.

"What's that you got there, brother?"

"Shut up," said Vladimir, kneeling beside Kirill. The Nightmare Man was too weak to put up a fight. The needle was punched into his shoulder muscle, a viscous serum delivered. He was barely aware of it.

Vladimir also had a medical spray, a type of liquid nitrogen. As soon as the cone of mist touched Kirill's wounds, they stopped bleeding.

"There. You might actually live to see another day!"

"What's going on? Talk to me, brother."

"You know what's going on. The zombies came."

"Who is doing this ... Who made the wall ...?" Kirill was barely conscious.

"Someone has to profit from every tragedy. Someone always does. I just happened to be on the winning side."

Kirill was shaking his head. "No ...we're meant to protect them ...the people ...you betrayed our own people."

"Are you fucking insane? This is Russia! We kill our own people if that's what it takes to get the job done."

"Help me ... let's work together ..."

"Not this time. I owe you my life a hundred times over, so I'm trying to pay you back now. The injection should reverse the zombie infection." Here, Vladimir laughed. "Hell, what do I know? It's purely experimental technology. For all I know, it may actually speed up the zombie infection. But the science guys said it would work. It gives you a chance, anyway."

Kirill was breathing weakly, eyes closed.

Vladimir said, "I'm leaving now, brother. I won't let you die like this, but I'm not going to betray my employer, either. I'm leaving for good this time. Just in case you ever do find me, you better have your hands very fucking high in the air, Kirill. I don't trust anybody." He got to his feet, agile and powerful.

He turned back to face the Nightmare Man. "But you were ... my friend. We killed children together. We fought for Russia side by side. That means something."

Then he vanished.

On the floor, Kirill's eyes slowly blinked open. His strength was returning.

HOTEL VIDGOF – the most expensive hotel in Chelyabinsk

Galloway stared at the giant screen. The live feed from Chelyabinsk had been cut off for almost one hour. The studio was running reruns of highlights of the events that had taken place in the city. The battle in the Tank Academy had been replayed from various different camera angles, the tech guys cleverly editing the footage to make it look like it was almost an entirely different battle. Galloway himself had tried his best to keep the audience at ease, bringing individuals out on stage and putting an arm around them and asking them who they thought would be the last contestant on Dom 3. He had even tried interviewing some of the security guards, but that had been an embarrassing act, demonstrating how pointless it was to put a man in front of the camera who responded to every question with grunts.

He gave his very best smile as he looked up to the studio audience. Two hundred rich people who had paid for the privilege of seeing the country's most exclusive show: Dom 3. Such a spectacle couldn't be televised or streamed, of course; hackers would uncover it. Government agencies from foreign countries that watched everything Russia did would be on that in a second. Human rights activists and bleeding hearts who hated to see the mistreatment of poor people would have been crying everywhere. Yeah, right. No one cared about the poor people they walked past them every day; the only time those anonymous people ever became important was when politicians wanted to parade their conscience on the world stage and show how much money they were giving to the Ukraine's poor, which was Russia's equivalent of what Africa was for the West. Galloway had seen poor people fishing through his garbage bin every morning looking for scraps to eat. Funny how the poor weren't important then, but when you tried to make them useful, tried to give their lives some meaning, then suddenly it became an issue.

No, the only way to conduct the show safely without any other country finding out was to have the studio right in the heart of the city, right where the action was. And what better venue than Hotel Vidgof, Chelyabinsk's most prestigious hotel? The guests were able to relax and retire to their hotel rooms when they wanted to, able to watch the action on their own private televisions while they sipped champagne and lay on their king-sized beds. Usually, of course, the guests preferred the large screen in the conference room, enjoying the atmosphere of Galloway's rantings and the energy of the audience.

Two hundred seats. The seats were simple but adequate, served by topless beautiful Russian girls who made ten years wages for working here for one day. They were microchipped and made to understand that if they ever talked about what they saw here, they would be executed. As Stalin used to say, "No person, no problem." The same methods were applied to the security guards.

"Ladies and gentlemen, I assure you our technicians are working to fix this problem right now," Galloway told the audience. "We'll have you watching the exciting escapades of the Nightmare Man again in no time. You can watch Sasha, and the Medved, and find out how the New Mafia is run with Masha and Rhyza having joint council –"

"Fuck you, moron!" shouted a Babushka from the third row. "We paid a lot of money to be here. More than enough to buy this studio. You get us what we paid for, right now."

Growing voices of agreement murmured together. Galloway lost his composure for a moment, scanning the faces of two hundred rich people who had gathered here today to watch Dom 3. The battle at the Tank Academy had drawn everybody from their hotel rooms to this improvised studio.

"Please, if you will just exercise some patience –"

"Boss, the Nightmare Man's here."

Galloway turned to his security captain, "What the fuck did you just say?"

The captain indicated a monitor that showed the lone Nightmare Man walking towards the studio from outside.

Galloway laughed. "This ought to be good! One guy against all the security in here. Alright, maybe we can turn this around after all. Get the cameras going. We're going to finish this show on a high."

By now, the audience was riled, many of the patrons standing, furious at the delays.

Galloway spoke, "We have an extraordinary surprise for you. It seems the Nightmare Man is here. He's found his way to the heart of the mystery. I'm going to go outside and meet the man himself now. Let's find out what he's got to say for himself."

All of a sudden, there was dead silence in the studio. There was a flat tone while the screen changed from endless reruns to an image of the Nightmare Man marching relentlessly towards the building, apparently unarmed.

Outside, Galloway spoke to the guards by the gate. "Any trouble, any fucking trouble at all you kill him, clear? I don't care if all he meant to do was scratch his nose; if he makes a move, I want him shot," he took a savage drag on his cigarette, "fifty times. Don't even let him come back as a zombie. Shoot him and make sure he's fucking dead."

He cast what was left of the cigarette into the bushes. There were seven guards, all armed with automatic rifles. That should be enough to stop even the Nightmare Man.

The cameraman appeared; he had been hastily awoken and had assembled his camera gear. "Ready, boss."

"Keep the camera on him, you fucking idiot. If you screw this up, I'll have you shot."

Galloway walked boldly towards the Nightmare Man, his cameraman struggling to keep up with the heavy gear.

"Hello, Kirill. It's a pleasure to meet you in person."

"Was it you? Did you put all those zombies in the city?"

"No, that was a side effect of the meteor storm, my friend. We had nothing to do with the actual outbreak of the zombies."

"You just happened to be filming."

The cameraman was within two metres of the Nightmare Man.

"It was an opportunity we couldn't pass up. But hey, you did extremely well. You made it this far alive! We lost track of you for a while there. Would you like to tell the audience what happened?"

"Hey, shithead," said the Nightmare Man, "there's a reason they call me the Nightmare Man."

"Oh, and what's that?"

"I'm going to kill you and everyone else who was involved in this. That's what I do. I kill the enemies of Mother Russia."

Galloway laughed. "I've got seven men with guns aimed at you. Just what is it you think you can do here?"

Kirill inhaled, eyes blazing at Galloway. Then he nodded. There were seven shots in quick succession. In less than two seconds, all seven of Galloway's men lay dead from sniper fire. They had all been killed by headshots.

Galloway noticed three Spetsnaz snipers stand up and slowly begin to approach them, sniper rifles carried with casual ease. These were the men who were meant to be guarding the perimeter to stop anyone from entering Chelyabinsk. He did not notice that The Sergeant, Vladimir, was not present.

The TV host looked back to the studio, a distance that seemed an incredibly long way in the snow. He looked into the clear eyes of the Nightmare Man. The cameraman was still filming.

"Let's go," said the Nightmare Man as he seized the television host. As they walked, Galloway noticed a group of people arrive behind the snipers. He couldn't be sure, but he thought it was the Medved, Karl, Masha and the others.

Back inside the studio, Kirill shoved the TV host in front of him. The audience was remarkably calm, probably believing this was part of the show. Kirill held a handgun as he moved Galloway to the centre stage.

Security guards appeared from the back of the audience area, running and holding compact machine guns before them.

Kirill called out to them, his voice amplified by the speakers. "Throw down your weapons and run away. If you do that, I promise you my snipers won't harm you. You have my word you will walk away from here alive."

The security guards hesitated, looking to each other, before ditching their weapons in the aisles and running for their lives.

The serving girls stood frozen, terrified, aware this wasn't part of the show.

Kirill addressed them, "*Deyushki, davay.*"

The girls never looked back as they fled the hotel.

Now Kirill and Galloway were joined by some of the other Chelyabinsk survivors, including Karl, Sasha, and the Medved. They were all armed.

"You saw everything that happened in Chel," Kirill said to Galloway. "Do you know where my brother is?"

"I do, but he's not here," said the television host, hands raised, finally realising the game was up. He knew his only hope was to keep talking and hope that something he said would inspire the Nightmare Man to allow him to leave with his life.

"I saw the video of him in Moscow. He was trying to escape Metro 2," said Galloway. "He was injured badly. I don't know how. But they found him when they sent in the containment teams. The whole thing was a mess … they never should have got out. I'm sorry, man, truly I am. Your brother didn't make it. He died in those tunnels. He became a zombie and he got rounded up like all the others."

"Is he still in Moscow?"

"No, most of the zombies from that outbreak were kept in the Moscow facility, in the Metro 2. Of course, they built better cells for them after they had escaped. But your brother was the only one who was sent out of there. He got sent to help start another containment centre."

"Where was he sent?"

"Zombie Containment Edinburgh," said the television host. "It's in the United Kingdom. It's a relatively new facility. They have had a couple of outbreaks already – the team there are fucking retards – but the clean-up crews were able to round the zombies up before any serious harm could be done."

Kirill released Galloway's jacket, talking to himself, "So the United Kingdom is keeping my brother as a zombie? I'll burn the entire fucking United Kingdom to the ground. People will be too scared to set foot outside their houses, but it won't matter. They're all as good as dead."

Masha asked Kirill, "What do you want to do with him?"

But it was Karl who answered. "I'll talk to him."

Sasha asked Karl, "Do … do you think you will be able to get any information out of him?"

The KGB officer paused for a moment. "I'll see what I can do."

Kirill met Karl's eyes. "Find out everything about these containment centres. By the sounds of things, this has spread beyond Russia."

The Bear said, "We don't know if there are any more cities in Russia like Chelyabinsk that have been taken over. Russia may now be a very dangerous place, more than normal. We could potentially have a lot of towns to clean up."

Masha said, "The Moscow centre might be a better place to start. We might be able to stop the problem altogether."

Karl smiled faintly at Galloway. "You'll be my masterpiece."

"Can I leave you to investigate the Moscow centre?" Kirill asked the Medved. "And if necessary, gain control of any infected towns that may be out there?"

"Sure, but why aren't you coming with us?"

"I will join you. But I'm going to visit Edinburgh first. In the meantime, my Spetsnaz will help you."

"Uh, sir," Sasha asked Kirill, "What would you like me to do?"

"You're an honorary Spetsnaz now. My guys will train you every day, teach you what it takes to be one of us. They'll look after you."

Sasha's eyes lit up. To become a Spetsnaz …

Kirill regarded the rest of his crew. "That just leaves one more problem. Now we need to deal with these people who enjoyed watching the suffering of Russian citizens."

The team moved toward the studio audience as one, casually raising their weapons. By now the studio audience had finally woken up to the danger. Various government ministers and lawyers cringed in their seats, begging for their lives, sobbing and sputtering tearfully.

The Chelyabinsk survivors levelled their guns at the studio audience.

They fired one shot each, and for each shot fired, one member of the audience fell. But they did not stay dead long. They shook back to unlife, pale eyes opening upon the world, and rose again, descending upon the screeching audience and ripping them apart, eating them alive, tearing out entrails, feasting on eyeballs and biting off faces, ripping limbs out of their sockets. There was nowhere to run, no way to escape, as all the doors had been locked by the Spetsnaz soldiers.

The screams were unending.

Later, the zombies who were able to move noticed the remaining humans standing calmly on the stage. The monsters hissed, as if expecting a trap, but then began to converge on the stage, desperate to eat the humans alive. It was the only thought they had.

The Chelyabinsk team did not retreat. Masha and Karl smiled as the horde got closer. They raised their weapons. Galloway had his hands tied behind his back now, his eyes wide – he had never seen a zombie up close. The Bear held an enormous machine gun casually, as if they were all going out for a drink rather than staring down a horde of the living dead. Anton held a pistol steadily, nervous but controlling himself. Sasha held a pistol in each hand, a look of amusement in his eye. Masha held her sniper rifle, ready. Karl grinned maniacally, pistol aimed at the crowd. The Nightmare Man regarded the approaching threat. His eyes were fierce, his jaw tense. He bared his teeth, raising a machine gun.

As the first zombies climbed the stage, the team of survivors opened fire, guns blazing, tearing the horde apart, brains and skull fragments flying everywhere. Bullets flew for what seemed like minutes and streams of spent casings hit the floor, bouncing, and were still.

PART 4
THE NIGHTMARE MAN

ZOMBIE CONTAINMENT EDINBURGH

The cell was more of a cavern. The walls were rough stone; water bled down them. There was almost no light, only a slim slice of illumination at the base of the door. No more than one person could fit comfortably into the cell. There was no bed, not even a toilet. There were shackles on the wall, and these lay open, the room's single occupant sitting against the wall beneath them. He wore stained clothes, like a battlefield surgeon. His skin was dirty, his nails black. He barely seemed to be alive.

The cell door opened and light bloomed inwards. The zombie on the floor was lit up; it reacted immediately, savagely snapped at the air. In a surge of motion, the zombie was on its feet.

The man who had opened the cell door said, "Aw, shit!" and quickly tipped out a plate of food onto the floor. He scampered back out the cell, a split second before the zombie could reach him. The door panel opened and the man stared back through at the zombie, who ignored the raw meat on the floor and was instead ruthlessly attacking the door, trying to reach the man on the other side. The man wore a blue baseball jacket; he was tall and bald. He breathed heavily, frozen before the zombie, perhaps waiting to be reassured that the glass would hold.

"I'm not afraid of you," he said after a few moments and walked away. The zombie ran violently against the door and the tall man jumped. He swallowed thickly and then walked away again, faster this time.

The light shone through the open panel and lit the zombie's face in hellish un-life. It was the face of Biter, the Nightmare Man's brother.

In the security room, Stevie sat on the couch drinking a bottle of beer. Stevie was a big guy, well over six foot tall. The beer he drank was called "Biter." It was spelled with two tees and one was crossed out, to change the word from "bitter" to "biter."

"How you enjoying your home brew, Stevie?" ask John, turning away from the monitors.

"I don't know, man," said Stevie. "I've been looking for a bottle opener for the past five minutes."

Stevie seemed to be seeing something in the air that John couldn't see, but that was normal when you drank Biter beer, which contained strong hallucinogens. At that point, Stevie was seeing faces in the walls. Earlier in the afternoon, he had been holding a conversation with a talking dog and a talking French cat smoking a cigarette.

John glanced back at the monitors. "That's Mick feeding the zombies. He'll be back in a minute."

Chris came into the room, carrying a handgun. He immediately put it back in its holster, then withdrew it again, like he was a gunslinger from the wild west.

"Be careful with that thing," said John. "You're going to shoot yourself in the foot one day."

"Nah, I'll be okay, I practice all the time," said Chris. He wiped his hands down the front of his military fatigues and adjusted his cap.

"Could do with a beer, though," he said.

"Great, just what we need," said John, "an idiot with a gun who's also hallucinating."

"Relax, I won't shoot you," said Chris, picking up a beer from the table. He couldn't find a bottle opener so his first instinct was to draw the gun again, holding the barrel to the top of the barrel to shoot it off. The gun was aimed through the bottle and directly at Stevie.

"Wait a minute," said Chris, "I could lose some beer if I do it this way. Better find a bottle opener. John, what happened to our bottle opener?"

"No idea, Chris. Maybe Mick took it with him."

"Well, when's he going to be back? It's beer o'clock here, and I always shoot better after I've had a few beers!"

"Yeah, well, just you stick with the handguns this time. I don't want you firing a machine gun again while you're under the influence."

"Yeah, yeah," Chris waved him away, "I learned my lesson. It was funny, though. I had to attend a corporate seminar on gun safety."

"Oh, right? And how did that go? You learn anything?"

"Nah, I had six beers before I went there."

Mick came back into the room. "The zombies are fed. We can relax for the rest of the day now."

"Good stuff, buddy!" said John. "I see Biter gave you a scare."

"Yeah, he's a psychopath."

Mick leaned forward to study the monitor screens. Most of them showed the inside of zombie cells, but several also showed areas like the cafeteria and vacant hallways. Mick was searching for one cell in particular. He saw one screen that said "Cedric." Inside was a giant man with long black hair wearing a kilt. His zombie face was painted blue. Another screen showed a Mafia gangster zombie there in a suit; he had cold black eyes that seemed to pierce the monitor screen. Another room held a young female zombie who looked like she had been beautiful in life.

Finally, he found it.

"There he is. Biter. That's one highly dangerous zombie," said Mick.

"I think they're all dangerous zombies," said John. "That's why they're in here."

"Well, okay, you know what I mean."

"Hey, Mick," said Chris, "You got the bottle opener?"

"Yeah, sure." Mick took the bottle opener from his pocket and threw it to Chris, who managed to catch it with both hands even though he was still holding the gun.

"Why did you take the bottle opener when you were feeding the zombies?" Stevie asked from the couch. Chris was opening himself a beer.

"I thought it was best I took it with me," said Mick, "for safety."

"Good thinking," said Chris, taking a swig of beer while he twirled the gun around his finger.

He stopped. "Shit, I better put the safety on."

Mick returned to the screen. Biter prowled about his cell, a caged lion. The Russian man looked like he had been strong when he had been alive.

"Hey, some mail arrived," said Stevie.

"Great," said John. "What have we got here? Fan mail? Or just bills?"

John took the envelope off Stevie. "This arrived last week! You should have given this to me earlier!"

"Sorry, man," said Stevie. "Looks important, though. That writing looks like it's from Russia."

"I think you're right, Big Stevie," said John, opening the letter. He took the letter out. His face was shocked.

"What's wrong?" asked Mick.

"Some guy called the Nightmare Man said he's coming to kill us. He said that Biter is his brother, and he's not happy that we're keeping him here like this."

"Is that him?" asked Stevie. "On the monitor over there? I can see someone walking towards us."
All eyes went to the monitor. The Nightmare Man was advancing up the corridor, carrying a machine gun. He seemed to be looking not only into the camera, but right into the room and into the very hearts of the men standing there.

Kirill raised the gun and fired once, destroying the camera.

There was only darkness.

"Come death, if you will: you cannot divide us; you can only unite us."
-Franz Grillparzer

"There is no death, because the wand of truth can change the driest bones to living things, and bring the loveliest flowers from stagnant ponds, and turn the most discordant notes to harmony and praise."
-The Aquarian Gospel

"In the democracy of the dead, all men are equal."
-Anonymous

"Death knocks impartially at the door of the poor man's shop and the prince's palace."
-Horace

"We cannot tell. We do not know. But whether death is an end or the beginning, we must not fear. For death is perfect rest and peace. The dead do not suffer."
-Robert Ingersoll

"What is death? A mask. Turn it and be convinced. See, it does not bite."
-Epictetus

"Your enemy is your greatest teacher."
-Buddhist saying

"Love your enemy not because he is your enemy but because beneath his enmity is the eternal fact of brotherhood."
-Harold Marshall

"It is easier to forgive an enemy than to forgive a friend."
-William Blake

"You carry heaven and hell with you."
-Ramana Maharshi

Thank you to my Russian friends, Sasha, Rhyza, Masha, and Kirill.

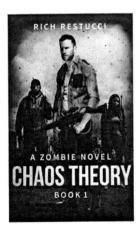

CHECK OUT OTHER GREAT ZOMBIE NOVELS

RUN
by Rich Restucci

The dead have risen, and they are hungry.

Slow and plodding, they are Legion. The undead hunt the living. Stop and they will catch you. Hide and they will find you. If you have a heartbeat you do the only thing you can: You run.

Survivors escape to an island stronghold: A cop and his daughter, a computer nerd, a garbage man with a piece of rebar, and an escapee from a mental hospital with a life-saving secret. After reaching Alcatraz, the ever expanding group of survivors realize that the infected are not the only threat.

Caught between the viciousness of the undead, and the heartlessness of the living, what choice is there? Run.

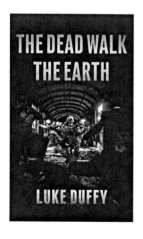

THE DEAD WALK THE EARTH
by Luke Duffy

As the flames of war threaten to engulf the globe, a new threat emerges.

A 'deadly flu', the like of which no one has ever seen or imagined, relentlessly spreads, gripping the world by the throat and slowly squeezing the life from humanity.

Eight soldiers, accustomed to operating below the radar, carrying out the dirty work of a modern democracy, become trapped within the carnage of a new and terrifying world.

Deniable and completely expendable. That is how their government considers them, and as the dead begin to walk, Stan and his men must fight to survive.

twitter.com/severedpress

CHECK OUT OTHER GREAT ZOMBIE NOVELS

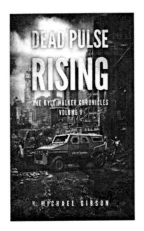

DEAD PULSE RISING
by K. Michael Gibson

Slavering hordes of the walking dead rule the streets of Baltimore, their decaying forms shambling across the ruined city, voracious and unstoppable. The remaining survivors hide desperately, for all hope seems lost.. until an armored fortress on wheels plows through the ghouls, crushing bones and decayed flesh. The vehicle stops and two men emerge from its doors, armed to the teeth and ready to cancel the apocalypse

TOWER OF THE DEAD
by J.V. Roberts

Markus is a hardworking man that just wants a better life for his family. But when a virus sweeps through the halls of his high-rise apartment complex, those plans are put on hold. Trapped on the sixteenth floor with no hope of rescue, Markus must fight his way down to safety with his wife and young daughter in tow.

Floor by bloody floor they must battle through hordes of the hungry dead on a terrifying mission to survive the TOWER OF THE DEAD

CPSIA information can be obtained
at www.ICGtesting.com
Printed in the USA
LVOW11s1808090517
533887LV00001B/107/P